POWER OF THE **P**

POWER OF THE

WHERE
HIP HOP
LITERATURE
BEGINS...

AUGUSTUS
PUBLISHING

© 2012 Augustus Publishing, Inc.
ISBN: 978-09825415-7-9

Novel by James Hendricks
Edited by Anthony Whyte
Design by Jason Claiborne
Photography By Milo Stone (Spicy Magazine)

Augustus Publishing paperback November 2012
www.augustuspublishing.com

IN MEMORY OF

My Grandparents: Frank and Estella Caster.
My Mom: Ernestine "Big Tina" Morris.
My Beloved Brothers: Alonzo "Zoe" Murphy, and Lenard "Len G" Garnett.
My young and talented cousin: Anthony "Jolly" Seals.

POWER OF THE

Acknowledgements

First and foremost, all praises due to Allah. I thank Him for the talent He has blessed me with and the opportunity to turn a negative to a positive. Second, I want to thank my family for still being by my side and loving me. To my beautiful wife and best friend, Marlisa Barnes, and my sons, Marrell Barnes (the responsible one), Marcus Barnes (the troublesome one) and Markel Barnes (the "too" smart one), and of course my step-son Marjuan Barnes (the smooth one), I want to thank you all.

The list of family and friends I would like to shout out has shrunk. Being locked up has given me clarity. Day by day, I find out truly who is true and who isn't. With that being said, I would like to thank my favorite aunt, Rhonda Ridgell, also my uncle David Caster, my granny, Ruth Brown, my cousins, Tasheka Russell and Shalondia Caldwell. Thank you's to my brother from another mother, Kory Jackson and family. Thank you to my brother from another father, Armondo Guzman Jr. and family.

These shout outs are for all those who kept it clean and is still keeping it real: Jalil Taylor, Terrene 'Boolash' Stokely, Eddie "Gingerbread" Fryer and Jason "Jr" Rowe. My God-mom, Diane "Mama J" Johnson, you are truly more than just a God-mom, Diane. You go above and beyond that title. I love

POWER OF THE

you. Jessica Randolph, I don't ask you for much, but when I do you always come through, thank you. Thank you my God- brothers, Wiley "Wally" Johnson and Benjamin "Bobo" Johnson. Thank you my God-sister, Tamikia Johnson and my God-children, Sammy Johnson and Sarai Johnson.

To all the soldiers fighting and struggling to come from under their unjust sentences, keep on doing it. Good work will pay off. Thanks to the following CCA members: Bobby "B.O." Suggs, Seantae "P-Long" Suggs, Aaron "Chuck" Davis, Terrence "T" Dilworth, Anthony "AJ" Jorge, Columbus "Nate" Malone, and of course my main man Terraun "Boo Rock" Price.

Thank you my long time associate, Jason "J-Boo" Best. Thanks Jacoby "Cold" Walker, Mike Mason, Karlos "Pudgy" Mayhew, Larry "Scotty Black" Scott and Anthony "Ant" Gibbs. The young, wild ones: Steven "Peanut" Rice, Stefen "Fatty Rice, Ronald "Ron-Ron" Seals, Michael Strong, Breion Campbell, Kerry "Little Kerry" Rice Jr. and Dontrell "Donnie Dollar" Rice.

God gave me the talent but you all gave me the opportunity. Thank you Jason Claiborne, Anthony Whyte and the entire Augustus Publishing family.

This story is dedicated to all women who keep their heads held high while chasin' 'em dollars.

JAMES HENDRICKS

POWER OF THE

CHAPTER ONE

"Roosevelt High presents to you, the graduating class of 2000…"

Cheers and applause filled the auditorium heralding the celebration that had officially begun. The announcement was made and students threw their caps in the air. They began hugging and kissing each other. In the midst of all the celebrating, Tameka Smith leaned over and gave Victoria Young the most passionate tongue kiss Victoria ever received.

"We're free! We're finally free," Tameka cheered.

A stunned Victoria could only muster a smile. Anna Marie Jones was about to say the words Victoria couldn't.

"Quit trippin', girl," Anna Marie said, laughing. "Don't be puttin' that girl on blast like that, you nasty ass heifer. Save that shit for the bedroom." Anna Marie coyly smiled.

"Shit, we grown now," Tameka chuckled.

"And what…?" Anna Marie asked, cocking her head to the side.

"And nothing," Tameka said, hugging Victoria around the neck. "We can do what we want when we want. Ain't that right boo?"

"That's right fo' real, fo real" Victoria said, smiling halfheartedly.

"Whatever," Anna Marie said, rolling her eyes. "So what we gon' get into tonight?"

"Business," Tameka said, getting serious. "We gotta come up with a way to get some money, some real money. Shit, I ain't trying to be working at no Baby Food Center for twenty years."

"But I thought we were going to party tonight," Anna Marie said, sounding disappointed.

"You know what they say," Tameka said, waving at some other excited students. "The future starts now."

"So where we gon' meet up?" Victoria asked.

"My house," Tameka immediately replied.

"What time?" Victoria asked.

"In about two hours," Tameka said, waving to other students. "That way we can get this out the way, and then have some fun, girl."

"Quit trippin', girl," Anna Marie said, laughing. "I'm with that. I'll see y'all in a few hours," Anna Marie said and sashayed through the door.

She left Tameka and Victoria standing, looking at the crowd in the auditorium. A heavy sigh escaped Tameka's lips.

"So is tonight our night, or what?" she asked, staring into Victoria's eyes.

"Fo' real though, I'm still not ready," Victoria said, squirming.

"Don't worry about it Victoria, I'm not trying to rush you into doing anything you don't feel like doing. You'll know when you're ready," Tameka smirked. "Shit, we grown now," Tameka chuckled. "I'll wait."

"Thanks Tam," Victoria sighed, feeling a little more comfortable. "Fo' real I kinda knew you'd understand. Right now, I better go start politicking at the damn foster home, if I'm gon' be able to stay out. Girl, I can't wait to get out on my own."

"Don't even think it, Vee. If things go according to my plan, you'll be out of there in a couple a months. Shit, we grown now," Tameka said with a chuckle.

"Fo' real, I sho' hope so," Victoria said, smiling, and hugging Tameka. "See ya later," she added, walking away.

"Okay girlfriend," Tameka said, staring at Victoria Young going down the block.

Tameka felt the pain of her best friend, watching her confident strut slowing to a death stroll. Victoria Young thought she was cursed from the day that she was born. Many had spoke of her mother being sweet, kind and a loving woman. Victoria never had the opportunity to experience the love and warmth. Her mother had died while giving birth to her, this haunted Victoria each and every day.

Her father, Rufus, raised Victoria on his own. With the love of his life gone, Rufus turned into an alcoholic. He provided Victoria with the basics, clothes, food and shelter. She could hardly remember any love shared between them. There were no happy times, Rufus's alcoholism worsened. When Victoria was seven years old, Rufus died in a car accident.

One night he had gotten really intoxicated and collided head on with a semi-truck. Victoria had no living family in Gary, Indiana. The welfare department was unable to locate any living family, and she was placed in foster care.

Victoria spent the next five years bouncing from foster home to foster family. Her case worker tried desperately to find a family willing to adopt her. She would move in with a family for a couple months, only to have them change their minds, and return her to the caseworker. Victoria became even more fragile with each rejection. It wasn't until her freshman year at Roosevelt High School that she began to loosen up and make friends.

Victoria met Anna Marie in gym class and they instantly hit it off. Anna Marie was already friends with Tameka. Thinking Victoria was a wild girl too, Tameka befriended Victoria. Victoria was just the opposite. To Tameka's surprise, Victoria was smart, quiet, shy and followed the rules. Tameka was pleasantly shocked to learn that Victoria wasn't interested in boys. Tameka was into girls and thought Victoria was also into girls. Tameka used their mutual disgust of boys in order to get Victoria's confidence.

Victoria also suffered from disturbing nightmares. The same recurring dream about a man having sex with her, kept her on edge. Even though she couldn't see the man's face, Victoria knew who the man was because his voice was familiar. She also knew it hurt when he was penetrating. Victoria attributed the dreams to her dislike for boys, but it was confusing because she didn't know if she was into girls.

At eighteen years old, Victoria stood five-three, weighing one hundred and thirty pounds. Her smooth, peanut butter complexion, made her dark hazel eyes dazzle. Long jet black hair, she wore straight back in a ponytail. Victoria was not interested in men, but was still longing for love and affection.

Things were different for her best friend, Anna Marie Jones. Anna Marie's mother was half black and half Indian. Her father was half white and half Puerto Rican. Anna Marie was the eldest of three children made, and the only girl. When she was ten years old, Anna Marie's father walked out on the family for a younger woman. Mrs. Jones didn't sit around crying, she told her children they should be thankful their father was gone. Anna Marie didn't understand what her mother meant, she didn't even care.

At a young age, she learned her looks would get her further than her brains. She was definitely using her looks to get what she wanted. Anyone who called Anna Marie was told, "Anything less than a key, you can't holla at me."

When she was twelve, Anna Marie was already dating boys sixteen, and seventeen years old. Boys would buy her clothes, shoes, jewelry and give her money. Early in life, Anna Marie decided she wanted money more than anything else. She clung to the edge of her virginity, until she turned thirteen. After her first sexual encounter, sex became Anna Marie's strongest weapon to get the money she wanted.

Growing up in the fast paced life of the streets, Anna Marie developed a violent temper. Always one to flaunt her jewels, she was hated by a lot of her peers. In eighth grade, Anna Marie started packing a box cutter for protection. She actually had to use it after Christmas-break in a fight. Anna Marie was beating up a hater when suddenly another girl jumped in the fight to help the girl. Pulling out the box cutter, Anna Marie slashed one of the girls across the face. Her violent reputation would follow her through high school.

Anna Marie's reputation with men preceded her to high school. Anna Marie didn't think their dollars long enough and didn't talk to the boys at her school. She continued dating older men who had lots of money.

Anna Marie was five foot-seven. Weighing in at one hundred and thirty pounds, she wore her long, black, silky hair cascading down the middle of her shapely backside. This feature wowed any man in her sector. Anna Marie's light green eyes were enhanced by her color of pure cream complexion. Deep dimples appeared in her cheeks when she smiled. Even though men catered to Anna Marie, she still kept a part-time gig at Lonnie's Music Store doing nothing.

She was supposed to be the cashier, but spent the hours listening to all the latest C.D's. Anna Marie would charm whoever was working with her into doing her duties. Life was sweet for Anna Marie. Now that she had graduated from high school, Anna Marie was planning on making it even sweeter.

Tameka Smith was the only one of the three girls who had a normal, stable home life. She grew up with both of her parents. Her father, John Smith, was an ex-military officer who owned his own security business. Amber Smith was her mother and taught eighth grade math at Tolleston Middle School.

She had two brothers and a sister. Tameka's older brother, Pete, was the closest to her. She loved her younger brother and sister, but thought they were spoiled brats and didn't like spending time with them. John and Amber loved and spoiled all their children, but Tameka felt because of her lifestyle, she wasn't appreciated.

Growing up, Tameka spent her early years watching cartoons and fighting boys. In school, Tameka looked for the easy way out. Every act was a about a scam. She befriended the smartest students in her classes in order to cheat off their tests, and copy their homework. Tameka didn't need any help when it came to mathematics. It was the one subject she was guaranteed to be the smartest student in class. Tameka would not only allow those helping her, but every other student to cheat off her paper. Her willingness to help others pass math was the reason no one exposed her little operation.

Tameka was a straight party girl with a wild side. If there was a throw-down happening, Tameka was there, shaking her ass the nastiest. It was widely known that Tameka was a lesbian. No man or boy had even the slightest chance at getting with her.

When she was twelve years old Tameka went away to summer camp. It was there that she became enlightened of her sexuality and preference. Tameka knew a lot of girls were experimenting with each other. Not wanting to be the only exception, she decided to join the fun. The experience of that summer went beyond her wildest sexual fantasy. Then and there she decided a man wouldn't do it for her.

Each passing year saw Tameka's attitude getting worse. She walked around with a box cutter. Just like Anna Marie, Tameka could fight, but knew females stuck together and couldn't be trusted. Unlike Anna Marie, Tameka never had to use her box cutter because her fight game was serious. She also had an ace up her sleeve, Pete. He had left behind a reputation for kicking serious ass. Boy or girl, Pete didn't discriminate. The teachers, even the principal, were all liable to feel his wrath. Tameka was five foot-six and weighed one hundred and forty pounds. She walked the school halls in baggy jeans and T-shirts like she was the owner. Everybody was always trying to be down with her team.

Her smooth, deep chocolate complexion showed off her light brown eyes. Tameka's long hair was always braided to the back. She never wore dresses and her hair was always undone. Tameka worked at Baby Food Center stocking shelves. Although Victoria also worked there, Tameka despised the job. Tameka was sitting in her home, thinking of the real reason she wanted to discuss the future with Victoria and Anna Marie. The doorbell disturbed her thoughts.

"Damn, it took y'all asses long enough to get here," she said, opening the front door.

"Quit trippin', girl," Anna Marie said, walking inside Tameka's house. "You know how them foster home people be trippin' on Victoria."

"Yeah, you should've seen Mr. Davis. He was on some other shit, fo' real. He kept going on and on about me wanting to stay out so that I could get my freak on," Victoria said walking pass Tameka.

"We know that ain't going on," Tameka mumbled under her breath. "Shit, we grown now," Tameka chuckled.

The girls went upstairs to Tameka's room. Anna Marie went straight to Tameka's room and turned the stereo on. Tameka immediately jumped up from her bed and turned the stereo off.

"We here to plan our future not get our party on," she said sternly. "We're grown now," Tameka sarcastically chuckled.

"Quit trippin'… My bad," Anna Marie said, joining Victoria on Tameka's bed. "So what's the plan?"

"That's what grown folks do, they talk and figure shit out," Tameka said, sitting back down on her bed. "I got an idea, but I want to see what y'all came up with."

Victoria glanced around the room, shaking her head. She then turned her head to the floor.

"Fo' real… I-I ain't came up with nothin'. I been too preoccupied with graduation and college. I haven't given it much thought," she said looking down.

"And what about you, Ms. Party Girl…?" Tameka asked, staring with a smirk on her face directed at Anna Marie.

"Me…? Quit trippin', girl," Anna Marie said. She paused before continuing. "I really ain't gave it much, much thought either." Seemingly in deep thoughts, Anna Marie played with her hair. "I mean we just finished high school. Let's just enjoy this accomplishment before we jump into another long-term commitment."

Tameka gazed around the room and shook her head. There was a long silence before she finally spoke.

"I can't believe y'all. I can believe you Victoria, but not you Anna Marie. We're all grown now. Our future is now."

"Quit trippin', girl. Why you can believe Victoria and not me, huh?"

Anna Marie asked, smacking her lips.

"Heifer, it ain't even like that. We grown folks here, and we can speak our minds," Tameka said smiling. "Victoria always said she was planning on going to college."

"Fo' real, I am goin' to college," Victoria said, beaming.

"My bad, Victoria is goin' to college. But you still gon' need some money. We're grown folks now."

Anna Marie stared blankly at Tameka. It was a clear indication that she was tired of the lecturing.

"Quit trippin', girl, and tell us all what you came up with, Mrs. Einstein?"

There was a lengthy pause. It was the kind of tense moment that could lead to an explosion. Tameka slowly rose to her feet.

"Stripping…" she announced.

"Quit trippin', girl. Bitch please!" Anna Marie blurted.

"We're all grown folks," Tameka said, walking to her dresser. "Strippers get pimped. They go out there gettin' fondled and shit and another muthafucka gets half for nothin'."

Again there was silence. Anna Marie and Victoria stared at Tameka, who was reaching into her drawer. She pulled out a sheet of paper.

"Quit trippin, girl…"

"Fo' real…"

"I ain't with that shit," Tameka said, looking at the paper. "That's why I came up with this."

"What is that?" Victoria asked.

"A summer hustle plan that's gon' get us right. We're all grown now, we need that dough," Tameka said, smiling.

Anna Marie read the piece of paper and laughed out loudly.

"Ass By The Pound…? What the… What the hell is that?"

Staring intently at one girl then the next, Tameka sat back down on her bed. She turned to her friends and pointed at each of them.

"That's you and me, that's us, we grown folks here…"

"Quit trippin', girl. I'll tell you, Tameka. You got vision but no place,"

Anna Marie said, looking at Tameka and shaking her head.

"I had to make sure that y'all was with it first," Tameka said, nodding.

"But wait a minute, fo' real, I thought you couldn't stand men?" Victoria asked sounding perplexed.

"Shit, we grown folks here. Me not likin' men ain't got nothin' to do with them green men that's in their pockets," Tameka chuckled.

"Fo' real, I don't know if I can have some man feeling on me," Victoria said unenthused by the idea.

"C'mon Vee, we grown, we can make a thousand dollars a night," Tameka said, grabbing Victoria's hand.

"A thousand dollars a night...? Quit trippin', girl," Anna Marie shouted. Her light green eyes were lit in surprised.

"Yes, I'm tellin' you. And we ain't even gotta do that shit every night. Just on weekends," Tameka assured the girls.

"I don't know 'bout you Victoria, but quit trippin', girl, I'm in," Anna Marie suddenly declared with a snap of her fingers.

"Fo' real, that's a whole lotta money," Victoria smiled, slowly shaking her head. "With all these broke ass niggas out here, how we gon' make that much?"

Tameka smiled sensing that Victoria was warming to the idea. She seized the opportunity to drop her ace.

"Don't even worry about nothing. Pete gon' take care of all the customers."

"Pete...?" Anna Marie spat in disgust. "Quit trippin', girl, why him?"

The smirk that took hold of Tameka's face said it all. She was offended by Anna Marie's reaction. Smiling calmly, she decided to let it go.

"Pete's cool with all the big ballers, okay? I ain't about to strip for no broke-ass-niggas and make hundred, uh maybe two hundred dollars a night. I'm tryin' a make G's and Pete can help make that happen."

"Fo' real, where we gon' do this at?" Victoria asked.

Tameka had anticipated that this was going to be the hardest part to sell, especially to Victoria.

"Hmm, I've been looking in the newspaper for a building we could lease. We can all put in a couple a hundred and we can ride from there."

"Fo' real, what about music equipment and all that jazz...?" Victoria asked.

"Don't worry V, it will pay off. Trust me, we grown folks now. This is an investment opportunity where we can't lose," Tameka said, again grabbing Victoria's hand.

"Fo' real, I'll do it," Victoria said, sounding reluctant. "But y'all know, I gotta pay my tuition and get books."

"Quit trippin', girl," Anna Marie said, hugging Victoria. "Your education comes first. I got you."

"It's settled then," Tameka said, smiling. "Me and Pete gon' start looking for a buildin' tomorrow."

"Good, now let's go party," Anna Marie said, jumping up from the bed.

"Fo' real..."

"We're all grown folks now... Y'all responsible for—"

"Quit trippin', girl."

CHAPTER TWO

Tameka was dead set on turning her vision into reality. Despite partying until four in the morning, Tameka managed to wake up early, and start her search for the perfect building to lease. She spent the early part of her day looking at buildings on the West side of town, but none of them caught her interest. They were either too small, too big, or needed too much work. She came close to leasing one of the buildings, but the location just wasn't right. Tameka was looking for a spacious building in a nice remote area. She couldn't afford to have anybody calling the police on her and her girls, especially since they didn't have a license.

Having no luck on the West side, Tameka decided to look for a building on the East side. The East side of Gary, Indiana, was once filled with flourishing businesses. However due to the steady rise in the city's crime rate, the once thriving East side businesses were shut down. The owners relocated their establishments, moving to other cities. Their exodus left a huge amount of empty buildings, some abandoned buildings, and decaying warehouses.

The East side provided plenty of buildings for Tameka to choose from. She didn't start out looking for a building on the East side because she thought there was no excitement. Because of all the secluded areas she could choose from, Tameka soon realized the East side was the perfect place. She came across the perfect building located on Ripley Street. It was the only building on that street and was away from the main road. Tameka had to lease the building for at least one year. It was the only thing she didn't like. The plan was to strip for one summer, not a whole year.

She signed the lease anyway. On her way back, she called Anna Marie, and told her the good news. They planned to meet at Tameka's house to further discuss their strategy. By the time she pulled up in front of her house, Anna Marie's car was already parked outside. Tameka got out the car and gave Anna Marie a hug.

"The building is right," Tameka said, smiling.

"Quit trippin', girl. Where is it at?" Anna Marie excitedly asked.

Tameka stopped smiling and stared at Anna Marie before continuing. She measured her words.

"It's on Ripley…" her voice trailed.

"Ain't that in Aetna? Quit trippin', girl," Anna Marie said, frowning.

"Yes it is, but I swear it's the right place," Tameka said with gusto.

The news seemed to blow Anna Marie away. She took a step back, and rested her curvaceous backside against her car.

"Damn, I just wish you could've found sump'n on the West side," she said, not hiding her disappointment.

"Me too, but the East side is the spot," Tameka said, leaning against Anna Marie's car. "We ain't got no license, no permit so we on some illegal shit. We can't just be all out in the open like that. We gotta be discreet 'bout this."

"You right," Anna Marie said, realizing there were laws. "Quit trippin', girl. You really think Victoria gon' go through this with us?"

"We're grown here," Tameka said, laughing. "I can't even imagine prissy-ass Victoria lettin' strangers feel on her."

"Quit trippin', girl. Look who's talkin'," Anna Marie said, laughing. "You're the king of the lesbians. I ain't met none as hardcore as you."

"We all grown folks here, what's that got to do with anything?" Tameka asked.

"You're talkin' 'bout Vee…? Quit trippin', girl, how're you gonna deal with men feeling on your ass?"

"I'm a be dealin' with it just fine," Tameka said, nudging Anna Marie. "My only motivation is all 'em dollars we gon' see," Tameka laughed while imitating counting money.

"Quit trippin', girl. Do you really think that we gon' make a lot of money?"

Tameka sighed and stared at Anna Marie for a beat. Then she put her arm around her friend's shoulders.

"Of course we gon' make a lot of money. Don't worry about it, Pete gon' take care of everything."

Anna Marie paused and turned to face Tameka, staring intently in her light brown eyes before speaking.

"I know you and Pete real tight, but do you really think he gon' come through?"

"I know he is. He's gon' get 'em comin' to see us, and the rest is on us," Tameka smiled, assuring Anna Marie.

"I have no problem strippin', but I still don't see how we gon' make thousands a night," Anna Marie said.

Tameka looked Anna Marie directly in her light green eyes. She could see concern written all over her face.

"When I say strippin', I mean strippin'. We gon' be butt-ass naked." Tameka saw the frown lines wrinkling Anna Marie's face. "Look, that's the only way we gon' get paid. The strippers that work in the strip club got to follow rules. You can't just show pussy. You can't show nipples. You can't let the men feel on you. You can't do this and you can't do that. With us, we can do whatever. Men will spend more with us than with them bikini wearin' bitches."

"Oh, quit trippin', girl. I get it now," Anna Marie said, smiling. "So, when we startin'?"

"Slow down, we still gotta get the equipment. You know music, a pole, tables, chairs, things like that. I say about a week or so, we'll be ready," Tameka laughed.

"Quit trippin', girl. The sooner—the better…"

"One more thing and you can't tell Victoria this."

Anna Marie's light green eyes got big as saucers before she asked, "What's up?"

"I had to lease the building for a year," Tameka whispered.

"If the money gon' be like you say it is. A year ain't shit. I'm tryin a retire by time I'm twenty-one," Anna Marie smiled.

"I hear ya girl."

The next couple of days found Tameka, Victoria and Anna Marie very busy. Before they went to their jobs they would clean the building inside out. The girls painted the inside walls black and gold. After they were satisfied with the cleanliness of the building, the three went bargain shopping for the tables, chairs and deejay's equipment.

They also purchased a pair of sliding poles. Pete didn't help with the cleaning duties, but Tameka had him install both poles. Pete also found and hired the deejay and a bartender. The two men were actually childhood friends. Pete was twenty years old, six feet tall and weighed two hundred pounds, they would also help him with the security for the girls. Pete's plan was only to invite patrons with lots of money, but he wasn't taking any chances with troublemakers.

Anna Marie lacked faith in Pete. She didn't believe he could actually get a lot of high rollers to come and spend money with them. Tameka however was confident in her brother because of his on-the-side hustle. Pete was one of the biggest marijuana dealers in the state and sold weed to a lot of big time dealers. It would be easy for him to sway them into spending some cash with his girls, instead of going to a regular strip club. Tameka was hoping he would fill the void.

Dark skinned, Pete had light brown eyes. He wore a neatly trimmed goatee and kept his hair corn rolled straight to the back. Pete had a reputation for killing anybody that crossed him, and Tameka was hoping his status would keep everybody in check.

The night of the grand opening finally arrived. A sparsely packed house was relishing feasting their eyes on these special girls Pete had bragged about. Boo Rock, the deejay and OJ, the bartender were in their set places. The girls were all there and ready except Victoria. A nervous wreck, she paced back and forth in the dressing room.

"Fo' real, fo' real, I can't do this. We don't even know the men out there," she said with trepidation.

Anna Marie was examining herself in the mirror. She flashed Victoria a nervous smile, shaking her head she said, "Quit trippin', girl. I'm nervous too. Shit, ain't none of us done this before. But we invested all of our money in this. We can't just give up."

"Yeah Victoria, we all grown folks here, we can't give up without at least tryin'," Tameka said, tying her shirt. "Dance when you all by yourself in front of the mirror."

"Quit trippin', girl, you not by yourself. So, let's just go out here and see how the first night goes. If it's not what we think then we can talk about sump'n else. We at least gotta give it a try."

"Fo' real... Fuck it, let's go," Victoria said, swallowing a shot of Hennessy.

The three women drank some more. Eventually they exited the dressing room, and entered the club, ready to work. Tameka was set, and went on stage first. She adopted the stage name, Black Diamond.

"That name matches my dark skin," she smiled to Boo Rock, the deejay.

Her intention was to let her costume impress the audience. Tameka was in a catholic school girl's uniform with her shirt tied around her slim waist.

"Here's the fiery Black Diamond...!" Boo Rock announced.

Tameka was disappointed when she heard the splatter of applause. It wasn't the welcome she had envisioned. Once she had taken off the uniform and was butt naked, the crowd started going crazy. Doing her dance routine, Tameka was on her back and opened her pussy up.

The crowd went crazy. Tameka blew their minds when she stuck one of her fingers in her pussy, and slowly lick the juices. The men started throwing twenties and fifties on the stage, cheering Tameka on. The large bills in front of her spurred Tameka to be daring. She smiled and continued to put on her show. The drinkers drank, and those who didn't drink rushed to order liquor from the bar, things were heating up.

Tameka drove the crowd wild with her onstage performance while Victoria and Anna Marie worked them for lap dances. Their work was real hard because Tameka had captivated the audience with an impressive performance. Victoria and Anna Marie managed to find a couple willing customers at the bar drinking.

Anna Marie jumped on the man's lap. Twisting and turning, she gave him one of the most erotic lap dances he ever received. Victoria lost her courage. She froze when a man attempted to shove a c-note in her G-string for services. Pete had to move in.

"Everything will be alright, Vee," he reassured her. "Just loosen up and do what you do. Gettin' money is just part of it," Pete advised.

The first lap dance felt like the most degrading thing she had ever done. It showed in her movements. She had no idea what she was doing and when the young man started to get an erection. Victoria jumped off his lap so fast you would have thought he tried to stick his dick in her. After the fifth lap dance, Victoria was a pro. She even went back to her first customer and gave him a lap dance for free. He paid for it anyway.

For about thirty five minutes Tameka kept the audience in awe, dancing on the stage. Customers would throw more money on the stage every time she was ready to leave.

"Stay up there!" they shouted throwing more bills onto the stage. "Yeah, we'll let it rain if you keep dancing. Catch up!"

Tameka shook her ass wild and fast on stage to an old 2 Live Crew classic, *Oh Me So Horny*. She seductively rubbed her hand over curves when an R&B joint played. Tameka's body shimmered with dripping sweat. She collected all the money and wrapped it up in her shirt. Instead of going back to the dressing room and cleaning, a butt naked Tameka walked straight into the crowd. Collecting more money, she proceeded to give the customer lap dances.

Tameka and Victoria entertained the crowd while Anna Marie was in the dressing room preparing to hit the stage. Because of her Indian background, she was using Pocahontas as her stage name. Clad in a skimpy deerskin outfit complete with a plastic hatchet, Anna Marie went onstage determined to outdo Tameka. The deejay dropped the first song on her list and Anna Marie launched her routine. Slow and sexy, Anna Marie showed the crowd some of her sex faces. Butt naked, Anna Marie was shaking her ass. The crowd was blown away, and Pete had to come closer to the stage to get a better look.

Pete and the entire crowd were drooling when Anna Marie got on her back and flashed an open shot of her pussy. She snaked her curvy body back to the middle of the stage. A plastic hatchet was there, and Anna Marie grabbed it. She teased the audience with a deep throat of the hatchet's handle. The attention of everyone in the house was riveted on Anna Marie. With mouths agape, they watched her enticingly slide the hatchet down her sexy naked body. Inch by inch she worked the hatchet's handle inside of her until she was masturbating on stage.

The crowd went out of control from Anna Marie's presentation of sexual pleasure. Tameka stopped giving lap dances to see what was driving the crowd into a frenzy. She was stunned by what her friend was doing. Even Victoria peeked out to see what Anna Marie was doing. She was also astounded to see her friend masturbating on stage. Both the audience and Anna Marie seemed to be having a lot of fun. Anna Marie was strutting around the stage picking up bills.

Victoria raced back to the dressing room in search of props to use. She was now forced to drop her good girl image, and come up with an act equal in impact to Anna Marie's. Victoria stood out of sight taking long deep breaths. Candy was her stripper name and she wore a two-piece, patent leather outfit with six inch, knee high leather boots.

Victoria borrowed a whip from Anna Marie's collection of toys, even though she had no idea how she was going to use it. Victoria thought the whip would spice her routine up if she used it right.

Anna Marie finished collecting the money and joined Tameka in the audience. The two had decided they would watch Victoria's routine. They wanted to see if Victoria would really take off her clothes in front of strangers.

The deejay made the announcement and dropped Cameo's song, *Candy,* and Victoria confidently strutted out cracking the whip. Anna Marie and Tameka stood in front of the stage cheering and laughing.

Victoria was quickly out of her outfit. She teased the audience by sliding the whip between her legs while dancing. Some of the men felt her routine and others didn't. After the performance Anna Marie had just given, they were expecting to see Victoria do more than dance.

"More! More! More!" someone in the audience started shouting.

Within seconds the chant had been picked up by the rest of the crowd, and everyone started to shout. "More! More!"

Victoria had to decide if she was going to give the crowd what they wanted. She knew she couldn't stick to this performance and wasted no time in giving it to them. Victoria cued the deejay to put on some slow music. She dropped down to her knees and ran the handle of the whip up and down her body. Finally she built up the nerve to go even further. Victoria rolled onto her back and stuck her middle finger inside her wetness.

Slowly, she started working her middle finger in and out her pussy until she was going full speed. Victoria was pleasing herself so well that she had forgotten all about the crowd. She kept working her finger in and out of her moistened pussy. Victoria took the whip's handle and rotated it around her clit.

The crowd went bananas, but Victoria's act had Tameka on the verge of insanity. She couldn't believe Victoria wouldn't have her, but would masturbate in front of total strangers. Victoria wasn't out of her sexual trance until she climaxed and heard the cheers of the audience. She slowly gathered her money then joined her girls in the crowd. The three young women spent the rest of the night giving lap dances, mingling with the customers, and getting paid. The men were raw, hungry and thirsty for more. They kept OJ, the bartender busy.

It was a little after two that Pete cleared the club. The girls counted their money. Tameka had thirteen hundred dollars and Anna Marie seventeen hundred. Victoria made the most money their first night, counting twenty-one hundred dollars. Pete charged the customers twenty dollars to enter and ended up with six hundred dollars. They pulled in twelve hundred from the bar and Pete made money providing weed to the customers. Tameka, Victoria and Anna Marie chatted while Pete paid Boo Rock and OJ, the bartender.

"I didn't think you had it in you," Anna Marie said to Victoria.

Victoria thought about it for a while. It was as if she was replaying the entire evening in her head. Then she smiled and said, "Fo' real, I didn't either. But when y'all started laughing at me and shit, I said fuck it."

CHAPTER THREE

The business venture was going well for the three young women. Not only did they survive their first weekend, but it was a success. After paying OJ, Boo Rock, Pete, and buying Hennessy for the upcoming weekend, they each made six thousand dollars.

The customers from the first night enjoyed themselves so much they spread the word about *Ass By the Pound*. It quickly became the moniker for Tameka, Victoria and Anna Marie. There were more new people showing up each night and this prompted Tameka to find other women willing to join them. Tameka realized the three of them wouldn't be able to cater to all the new customers and that would eventually cause problems.

Anna Marie was against the idea of bringing in more women, but after Tameka explained that because of the growing crowd, they wouldn't lose money, Anna Marie went along. Tameka started working on Victoria after witnessing Victoria's first act on stage. She couldn't get the image of Victoria climaxing in front of everyone out of her head. The freak was now coming out of Victoria, Tameka thought. She had been patient, but she felt it was now time for the two of them to finally get together.

Tameka and Victoria were drinking coffee on their break at Baby Food Center. Even though they made a lot of money over the weekend, the three women decided it would still be best to have a legitimate job. Victoria had her head down on the table.

"What's up, girl? Why you so quiet?" Tameka asked.

"Fo' real, I'm just tired," Victoria yawned.

"Tired of work, or tired of that foster home?" Tameka asked.

"That damn foster home," Victoria said, rising. "Fo' real, if I didn't have to get me a car, I'm tellin' you, I'll be lookin' for a place of my own."

"We all grown folks here, so what's stoppin' you?" Tameka asked.

"Duh, I just said I need transportation first," Victoria said, shaking her head. "Let's not forget I'm doin' this on my own. I don't have a mother and a father to buy me a car or anything for that matter," she said, referring to Tameka's parents.

"But it aint gotta be that way," Tameka said, sitting her cup down. "You got me."

Victoria looked Tameka directly in her eyes and asked, "So, what are you saying, exactly?"

She knew exactly what Victoria was implying, and Tameka wore a wry smile across her face. She spoke with increased intensity.

"Look, we're friends first, but we're also grown folks," Tameka said, staring intently at Victoria. "You want to get out of that foster home and I want to get away from the rug-rats. If we go half on a place you can still get your car. You get everything you want and I get what I want."

"Fo' real, what exactly do you want?" Victoria asked, looking skeptical.

"To get away from my family," Tameka said convincingly. "I know what you think. And it ain't even about that. It ain't about sex. We're grown folks here, I can wait for that. When you're ready for any sex, you'll let me know."

"Fo' real... Okay, I'm with it," Victoria reluctantly agreed.

Victoria didn't think Tameka was a bad person. She just wasn't ready to sleep with her. Victoria's issues had nothing to do with Tameka. She didn't know if she was straight, lesbian or bi-sexual. Victoria knew she would have to deal with her sexual preference one day, she was hoping that day wouldn't come sooner than she expected. Sharing an apartment with Tameka might work out.

While Victoria thought about the decision, Tameka wasted no time in looking for an apartment. Her assertiveness made Victoria wish she had not agreed to the plan. That same evening, Victoria told Anna Marie that she had agreed to share an apartment with Tameka, Anna Marie informed her that she would've loved to share a place with her.

Victoria was feeling frustrated for not having enough patience. She got off the phone and screamed at the top of her lungs. Anna Marie had said that Tameka's only reason in wanting to live with Victoria was because she wanted to get into her panties. Victoria assured Anna Marie that she would be careful, and if it didn't work out the two of them would get a place.

It was Thursday, one day away from another weekend. Tameka had found a two bedroom apartment in Gary's Glen Park area, but had not found another woman to join them. She had been so focused on finding an apartment she didn't even go looking for another woman. When Tameka showed Victoria the apartment, Victoria was really impressed.

They walked in and inspected the two bedrooms, one bathroom, living room, dining room with a full kitchen. The apartment sat directly across the street from a community college, because of constant patrolling by campus security, the area had a low crime rate. They had found their refuge, but decided to wait until after the weekend to furnish the place.

Tameka, Victoria and Anna Marie found the work week long and boring. After their first weekend dancing, the everyday grind lacked the excitement they felt on stage. Tameka, the most restless, couldn't wait for Friday night to come. She yearned to hear the crowd and have some fun. Friday night finally came. The young women had so much fun entertaining the largest crowd they ever had, they lost track of time. Before they knew it Pete was yelling "Last call…" Then before they realized it, they heard Pete shouting, "Its closing time…"

Friday had come, and it was leaving as quickly. Some of the patrons felt they didn't receive enough attention. They were letting their disgruntled voices heard and Tameka came up with a plan. She told Pete to extend the closing time two extra hours. The crowd was very happy and the girls made more money in that one night than they made in two nights combined the previous weekend.

After the last customers had filed out, all three exhausted girls plopped down in chairs. The night's activity left them drained. Victoria and Anna Marie were ready to pass out and go to sleep. They decided to leave everything the way it was. They would come back early to clean, and set up for Saturday night.

Saturday rolled around and all the girls dragged themselves to the club sporting bags under their eyes. Anna Marie watched Victoria attempting to put on a pair of rubber gloves before speaking.

"Quit trippin', girl. Last night took a lot out of me. I'm tired as hell."

"Fo real, me too," Victoria said, donning a pair of rubber gloves. "Fo real, I feel I'd been better off just staying woke."

Anna Marie shook her head. "Quit trippin', girl. I don't know about all that. A little sleep for me is better than no sleep."

"Fo' real, my ass is tired too, but we needs to get to cleaning," Victoria said, standing on shaky legs.

They started cleaning at a slow pace, but once fully awoke, the three business partners breezed through the cleaning of their establishment. They were setting up the chairs when a young woman walked in.

"May I help you?" Tameka asked.

"I strip at Club Extasy and a couple of the customers told me y'all was looking for more girls," the woman answered, stopping in front of Tameka.

"You kinda on the thin side to be strippin' ain't you?" Tameka noted, eyeing the woman from head to toe. "And you do know that we call ourselves Ass By The Pound, don't you?"

"How's this?" The slim woman smiled.

Turning around, she displayed all of her assets. Her backfield was well stacked with a butt that would give Tameka, Victoria, and Anna Marie a run for their money.

"What you said your name was...?" Tameka quickly asked. She raised her brow, pleasantly surprised. "When can you start...?"

"The name's Renee," she answered, extending a hand. "I can start tonight."

"This ain't like no ordinary strip club. We ain't got no rules, so sometimes things be gettin' pretty wild up in here," Anna Marie said, shaking Renee's hand.

"I got three older brothers, so I think I can handle myself pretty well," Renee chuckled.

"Quit trippin', girl..."

"Hi, Renee, I'm Victoria. Fo' real you're gonna be fine. I'm the shy one, and if I can do it, I know you'll do great."

"I'll definitely be tryin'," Renee said, smiling.

The women finished setting up everything for the night's performances. They sat around just kicking it. Tameka, Victoria and Anna Marie got a chance to know Renee. It was also a time for Renee to get to know her coworkers. Tameka was having a hard time figuring out what place Renee should dance. At first she was going to have Renee start the night off by going first, but Victoria was against it.

"Fo' real, she doesn't really know the crowd like we do," Victoria said. It was a good point and everyone listened as Victoria continued. "She should go last or next to last."

"I agree," Anna Marie said.

"We'll do our routine and let the audience warm up to Renee," Tameka said.

The audience would see Renee's routine at the end of the night. She would dance last. It would also give Renee an opportunity to see how her coworkers got down.

"The closer is the most important piece of the show," Tameka said to Renee. "You always gotta leave the audience happy and satisfied. We grown and we know when you not satisfying the customer, he might not show up again. This means less money for the next night," Tameka said.

"You're sure right about that," Renee said, nodding in agreement.

"Quit trippin', girl. I gotta get sump'n to eat. I'm famished."

"Fo' real, me too..."

The women went to a restaurant not far away and ate heartily.

Saturday night came and the women's club was officially jumping. The crowd was even bigger than the night before, but it wasn't because of the ballers, it was because of the women who were present in the audience.

Renee was used to seeing women in strip clubs, but Tameka, Victoria and Anna Marie weren't. The three didn't know if the newfound clientele were actually customers or the competition, checking them out.

Tameka earned everyone's confidence when she was paid extremely well by two of the women customers after giving them lap dances. They figured their competitors wouldn't pay them anything, and certainly wouldn't have been as generous as the two women who just paid Tameka.

That night, things progressed strangely. The female customers seemed to be competing with the male customers for the dancers' attention. Tameka was turned on by the presence of the female customers. It showed in her lap dances, and her performance on stage. While she catered to the women, Victoria concentrated on the men.

Victoria did try to get some of the female patrons' money. She couldn't stand the feeling of another woman's breasts pressed against her back. Soft hands between her legs, and soft voice in her ear was too much for Victoria. She decided to make as much money as possible from the male patrons.

Anna Marie was amused by the customers. She liked the way both men and women threw money at her. Anna Marie was strictly about the penis, but had no problem getting the females' attention and money.

Renee handled the situation like a professional. She was completely detached, moving from customer to customer, and making her money. She flirted with the women in the same manner she did with the men. This led Tameka, Victoria and Anna Maria to think that Renee was bisexual. They kept their thoughts to themselves and huddled to watch Renee's performance.

She chose the stage name, Mercedez, because her plan was to one day own a Benz. Renee patiently waited in the dressing room for Boo Rock to call her to the stage. Her long, black hair clung to the caramel skin of her shoulders. She wore honey colored contacts and was definitely on the slim side.

Her breasts were small compared to the other dancers, but what Renee lacked on top, she made up for it below. Her slim waistline showed off her lithe and trim figure. Her shapely structure confirmed that she was a dancer. Breathing slowly, she rotated her five-nine, one hundred and thirty pound frame. After watching the other dancers' routines, Renee knew she had to come with something the crowd had never witnessed before. Renee was planning to bring the house down.

Boo Rock introduced her, and she stormed the stage with confidence. She didn't go all out with her costumes like her coworkers had done. Instead, Renee wore white G-string outfit complete with six inch high white leather boots.

Immediately, the crowd was intrigued because Renee worked the two poles like she was born on them. She jumped on one pole, and slid down it slowly with her legs spread eagle, flashing the crowd with the imprint of her pussy. She used the other pole to spin around and do flips.

Patrons cheered loudly when Renee got into her seductive routine. They went wild when she started peeling off her costume. She untied her top exposing small breasts.

The crowd became raucous and started to shout, "More... More!"

Renee willingly obliged, shaking off her right boot then the left. With her back to the audience, she bent over in the middle of the stage, shaking her fat shiny bootie. She slowly pulled her G-string down.

Her pussy glistened in the stage lights while the audience went bananas.

Renee turned around and threw the piece of garment in the rowdy crowd. Strutting to the end of the stage, she got on her back and wrapped her legs around a faithful customer's neck, pulling him toward her pussy.

The customer leaned forward attempting to lick Renee's exposed pussy, but she held out her hand stopping him. The man reached into his pocket and quickly came up with a stack of hundreds, letting it rain on Renee. After she safely tucked the money away Renee got in position so the willing customer could bring her pleasure.

The rest of the night was easy for the dancers and they made a lot of money. When all the customers had exited the club, the women sat around counting bags filled with dough.

"Girl, I can't believe you let that nigga eat yo pussy like that," Tameka said.

Renee momentarily stopped counting her money. She looked up at Tameka and said, "You told me to leave the customers happy."

"Quit trippin', girl. Happy is one thing, full is another," Anna Marie laughed.

"Don't hate on the playa," Renee smiled.

"Hate the game," Renee and Victoria chorused and high-fived.

They went back to counting up the night's loot. For two hours, they cleaned up and made jokes about the night's events. Renee did extremely well for her first night. Because of the pussy eating stunt, Renee was the big winner for the night. She made forty-five hundred dollars.

The weekend flew by and before the ladies knew it, Monday morning was on them. Victoria took the day off, and shopped. Tameka took time off and got the furniture in her apartment organized. Although Tameka and Victoria decided to wait until after the week to start looking for furniture, Tameka just couldn't wait. She spent the last four days buying furniture behind Victoria's back, and was ready to surprise her with their newly furnished apartment.

Victoria found a 1996 four door Ford Taurus for $7000. The price was a little more than Victoria wanted to pay but she fell in love with the black and burgundy car, plus, it had low mileage. Victoria drove off the used car lot feeling really good. The car was the first of many more goals she planned on accomplishing.

Tameka waited at her parent's home for Victoria. She had called and told Tameka that she was on her way. She wanted to show her something. Tameka sat on her parent's front porch smoking a blunt with Pete with her mind on Victoria. Pete was in the middle of telling Tameka a joke when Victoria arrived. He didn't recognize the car, stood up, and pulled out his .45 Desert Eagle. Victoria got out just before he was about to send a bullet in the car's direction.

"Oh shit!" Tameka screamed. "Look at my girl. She's looking soo grown."

"You almost just got your shit shot up," Pete said, putting his gun back in his waistband.

"Damn, you hatin like that," Victoria said, giving Petea hug.

"Nah you know I ant't gon' hate on nobody. I just didn't know that was you," Pete said, returning the hug.

"Fo' real... It's all me," Victoria said, beaming.

"You should be proud of yourself. You got that all on your own. Today must be your lucky day because I got something for you," Tameka said, giving Victoria a hearty embrace.

"What?" Victoria asked.

"You drive, and I'll navigate," Tameka smiled.

The two women got in Victoria's car and left. Victoria was confused when their stop ended at the apartment.

"What are we doing here?" Victoria asked.

Tameka got out the car and said, "C'mon and find out."

Victoria got out the car and followed Tameka into the building. She was definitely surprised when Tameka opened the door.

"When did you do all this?" Victoria asked, after getting over the shock.

"I've been putting in overtime to get outta that house. Now we straight, you got your car, and we got our place," Tameka said, closing the door. "You must have had a long day, why don't you go and take a long hot bath."

"I ain't got no clothes," Victoria said, admiring the living room set.

"Yes you do," Tameka said, pulling Victoria toward the back of the apartment. "What's mine is yours. Pick out whatever you want," she added, pointing at the clothes sprawled out across her bed. "I'm a go run you a bath."

Victoria was too tired to argue. She went straight to the bed, and picked out an extra long white T-shirt. Once the bath water was ready, Tameka went to the bedroom and got Victoria. Victoria was tired and slowly made her way to the bathroom. The water was warm and soothing. Victoria fell asleep in the tub.

Taking advantage of Victoria's absence, Tameka went to the kitchen and grabbed the bottle of Dom Perignon she bought early that day along with two champagne glasses, and took them back to her bedroom. She lit scented candles placed around her bed, and turned on *Twelve Play*, her favorite R Kelly CD. She turned the covers on her bed then went to check on Victoria. Tameka figured that Victoria would be too tired to put up much of a fight, and she had set the mood where Victoria couldn't refuse.

She knocked on the bathroom door. There was no response, and she opened the door. The sight of Victoria asleep in the tub brought a smile to Tameka's face. She walked inside the bathroom and rubbed Victoria's forehead.

"Hey sleepy head, you alright…?"

"I guess I was more tired than I thought. I'm all right now," Victoria said, sitting up in the tub and exposing her perfectly sized breasts.

"I hope so, because I know we gon' kick it," Tameka said with a smile.

"I'll be there in a minute," Victoria said, standing up in the tub.

Tameka had more than an eyeful, and left the bathroom after seeing Victoria with suds all over her naked body. She hurried to the kitchen, and grabbed a bottle of Seagram's Gin. Tameka guzzled it.

She had seen Victoria nude many times at the club but never while it was only the two of them. Tameka put the bottle of gin down, and returned to her room. After a couple of minutes Victoria appeared wearing the oversized

T-shirt.

"I know you should be nice and rested," Tameka said, reaching for the champagne. "Have a drink with me."

"I already know what you trying to do," Victoria said, sitting on the bed.

"And what am I trying to do?" Tameka asked, filling Victoria's glass to its capacity.

"Seduce me," Victoria said, taking the glass of champagne and drank it down.

The two sat around listening to R Kelly, 112 and Jagged Edge while they finished the Dom. When Jagged Edge's *Gotta Be* played, Tameka jumped up.

"That's my song," she said.

"Fo' real...? Nah heifer, you know that's my jam," Victoria said, jumping up and seductively dancing.

Tameka stepped back and let Victoria do her thing. She noticed Victoria was dancing without any panties. Tameka danced her way in front of Victoria and kissed her lips. Victoria pulled away. She was about to speak, but when she opened her mouth, Tameka stuck her tongue in Victoria's mouth. Tameka pulled Victoria's body closer, and started rubbing her hands all over Victoria's bare ass.

Her hormones were racing, and champagne didn't make it any better. Tameka eased Victoria down on the bed and started pulling up the T-shirt.

"No plastic dicks," Victoria said, stopping her.

"Whatever you say," Tameka said, pulling the T-shirt over Victoria's head. "Hmm, beautiful," Tameka said, looking down and admiring Victoria's naked, sexy curves.

Running her index finger up and down Victoria's stomach slowly, Tameka gazed in Victoria's eyes. Then Tameka leaned down and softly kissed Victoria's swollen lips. She opened her mouth, allowing Tameka's tongue to wander inside.

Victoria surprised Tameka by pulling her on top. The two women passionately kissed for a minute. Tameka began massaging Victoria's breast, first the left then the right one. A couple minutes later Victoria found

Tameka's lips all over her left ear.

"You're soo beautiful," Tameka whispered, sucking and nibbling on Victoria's ear lobe.

Tameka moved down, licking and sucking on Victoria's neck. Victoria was moaning in pleasure when Tameka moved to her breasts. She cupped Victoria's right tit in her hands and ran her tongue around the hardened nipple. Tameka's tongue moved from the nipple area to the side of Victoria's breast where she began sucking.

"Oh yes, yes, ah yes," Victoria moaned.

Tameka focused on the side of Victoria's breast a little while longer before running her tongue to Victoria's nipple. She stuck Victoria's tit in her mouth, slowly pulling her mouth off it. She bit down softly on Victoria's nipple before doing the exact same thing to her left breast.

Victoria's stomach was quivering when Tameka ran her tongue up and down her torso. Tameka traced her tongue along Victoria's stomach, and raked her fingernails down the sides of her body.

Tameka licked and kissed Victoria's belly button, but her mind was focused on a spot further south. She held out, but once Tameka got a whiff of Victoria's pussy, she couldn't wait any longer. She had to taste it. Tameka parted Victoria's leg and instantly became intoxicated by her scent. She could see Victoria's juices already leaking out her pussy lips. She stuck out her tongue, and ran it over Victoria's outer lips.

"Hmm, tasty," Tameka said, parting Victoria's pussy lips.

"Ooh yes!" Victoria screamed when Tameka's tongue made contact with her clit. "Oh, don't stop. Fo' real... Don't stop!"

Tameka glanced at the excited face of Victoria. It made her smile while taking a break from sucking Victoria's clit.

"You taste soo good. I ain't gon' ever stop."

Tameka stuck her face back down between Victoria's legs and finished what she started.

"Oh yes oh yes," Victoria screamed, erupting.

By the time Tameka was through, Victoria climaxed three more times.

Tameka then climbed back on top of Victoria and tried to kiss her. Victoria turned her head and rolled over. The spent friend and housemate fell into a deep sleep. Tameka wore a look of confusion all over her frustrated face. She finished the bottle while masturbating to the sound of *Jagged Edge*.

CHAPTER FOUR

Summer was winding down but the four young women weren't. Tameka, Victoria and Anna Marie had already exceeded their own expectations. Renee wished she had joined them sooner. The majority of their customers were drug dealers and the money they made often wavered from weekend to weekend. As with most illegal activities, drug dealers didn't last. This meant that the women often were sometimes disappointed with the money they made. Even when some of their customers were locked up the women still made at least a thousand dollars.

The steady cash flow clouded Tameka's judgment. She made the proposal that they quit their day jobs and only do their dancing gig. Anna Marie was against the idea, but Victoria was the one who really pointed out why.

"Fo' real, we need to keep our nine-to-five for credit purpose, taxes, insurance and more importantly, to show where some of this money is coming from," Victoria said.

"That's true," Tameka agreed.

They all decided to keep their day jobs. Anna Marie got Renee a job working at the record store with her. Financially, things were going well for the young ladies, but on the personal side, some were suffering.

On the surface Tameka and Victoria appeared to be happy, but inside they weren't. Ever since that night the two had sex, Victoria had been acting different toward Tameka. At the time Victoria enjoyed herself, it showed in how many times she climaxed. Afterwards Victoria would get sick to her stomach, every time she thought about their sex episode. She never discussed her true feelings with Tameka. She decided instead to always stay sober when she was alone with Tameka. Her response left Tameka confused.

Tameka didn't understand why Victoria became so withdrawn. She knew Victoria enjoyed herself the night she ate her out, but that was also the same night Victoria's behavior seemed to change. Tameka tried reaching out to Victoria, but every time she asked, Victoria told her that everything was cool. Tameka decided to give Victoria the space she needed to sort out what she was going through. Tameka knew she had skills with her tongue, and that it was only a matter of time before Victoria came back.

Anna Marie continued to manipulate men into buying her whatever she wanted. Stripping not only allowed the big spenders to know who she was, but allowed her to find out who they were. One by one Anna Marie would pick a customer to cater to her needs. After she used them for what they were worth, Anna Marie would let them down easy and move on to the next one. Anna Marie was still using her looks to get what she wanted.

Victoria was preparing for community college. With her first class only days away, she was buying the materials she needed for her classes. Victoria planned her class schedules to accommodate her work hours at Baby's Food Center, and her weekend gig. She was aware that she was spreading herself thin, but also knew it would pay off in the end.

The night before Victoria's first class Tameka, Anna Marie and Renee gave her a surprise party. A lot of their customers showed up to support Victoria and many of them gave her extra money for school. Everyone was having a good time except O.J. The bartender was sitting at the bar by himself when Tameka walked over to him.

"What's up, O.J...? Looking like you not having a good time?"

The bartender sat his drink down and painfully looked up at Tameka. He swallowed hard before speaking.

"Ain't no snow up in here," he murmured.

"Snow…?" Tameka echoed with confusion written on her face. "I didn't know you fucked with cocaine."

"Nah Tameka, I ain't talkin' 'bout no drugs, girl. I'm talking 'bout some white girls," O.J. said, laughing.

Tameka smacked her lips. "You got all these bad-ass, black bitches up in here and you talkin' 'bout a white girl?"

"Yep," O.J. said, picking up his glass. "Hey, you know I always say, 'if it ain't snowin' I ain't goin'.'"

"That's real sad, but I might have sump'n for you this weekend," Tameka said shaking her head.

"Oh yeah," O.J. said, beaming.

"Calm your ass down," Tameka said, patting him on his back. "First, I gotta check her out."

"I hope everything go well. A white girl will surely brighten the atmosphere up in here," O.J. said, turning his drink up.

"I got you, boo," Tameka said, sashaying off.

The rest of the night was spent having fun. The women partied with their customers until the wee hours of the morning. When the party was over, all the dancers and bartender cleaned the place, before leaving.

Wednesday came and Victoria was officially a college student. She had already been to two classes, already there was homework due for one of the classes. Victoria was supposed to accompany Tameka to a strip club to check out the white girl, but she used school as an excuse not to go. Tameka didn't argue she went alone.

The strip club was called Simply Beautiful. It was located on the corner of 15th and Taft. Tameka was there to meet and watch a white dancer. Tameka sat down at a table and noticed there were twelve customers. The club was dead. Couple tables away from where Tameka sat, a thick white girl was talking to an older black man. Tameka figured the woman to be Snow Bunny, and decided to sit back and watch.

Tameka had been sitting at her table for an hour watching the woman move from customer to customer in hopes of giving a lap dance. The woman was headed in Tameka's direction when the DJ called her to the stage. The dancer was indeed Snow Bunny. Tameka sat at her table watching Snow Bunny's style of dance. She did a lot of Renee's routine in her performance. There were acrobatic moves, but she also had some of Tameka's wild and fiery ways in the routine. Tameka sipped on a glass of Hennessy, and decided to give Snow Bunny a chance. Snow Bunny was finished dancing, and Tameka called her over to the table.

"Have a seat." Tameka said smiling. "We need to talk."

"About…?" Snow Bunny asked, sitting across from Tameka.

"A job," Tameka said, before she turned up her glass.

"I got a job," Snow Bunny said flatly.

"Look at this place," Tameka said, scanning the club. "This ain't no job, this is slavery. I'm offering you a chance to be down with my team."

"And what team is that?" Snow Bunny asked defiantly.

"Ass By The Pound," Tameka said proudly.

"Oh yeah, I heard of y'all," Snow Bunny said, nodding. "Y'all supposed to be getting some major paper."

"Indeed, we are," Tameka said, reaching into her pocket for a piece of paper. She handed it to Snow Bunny. "And so can you. If you want, give me a call before Friday," Tameka said. Then she stood up and continued. "And your name is now Bambi," she said with a cocky smile.

Bambi called and O.J. proved to be right. The first two weekends, Bambi received a lot of attention and a majority of the customers' money. Victoria and Anna Marie were not bothered by the decline in their money, but Tameka and Renee were.

Renee's problem was two-part. The first part of the problem had to deal with the fact that a white woman was making more money than she was. The second part was jealousy, Renee was jealous of Bambi's 36-25-40 measurements. She couldn't believe how she was stuck with her slim figure while a white girl was blessed with a body she wanted to have. Tameka was jealous of Bambi, but not because of Bambi's figure. She hated to be outdone, and Bambi was definitely outdoing Tameka without even trying.

It was Sunday night, and Pete was on a mission. He kept his eyes on Bambi's every move. He knew she was fucking some of the customers because they had told him. Not only did they tell him she was fucking, but they bragged about how good she was. Pete didn't want to be excluded anymore. He watched Bambi go into the dressing room, and followed her.

"Damn Pete, you scared me," Bambi said, jumping.

"You should be," Pete said, sounding serious.

"Pete, what're you talking about?" Bambi asked, walking over to the sink, and turning the water on.

Pete grabbed a towel and walked over to Bambi. "I'm talking about you slangin pussy on the side."

"What?" Bambi said, confused.

"You fuckin' every customer that comes through here," Pete said, wiping Bambi's backside off. "You mixin' our business with your personal business."

She knew what Pete was talking about, but still was a little confused. "I don't get it. If we have no rules, why can't I sleep with whomever on the side, and get a little more money in the process?"

"I understand you only been here couple weekends, but it's already understood you don't fuck the customers. Tameka will let you slide once, maybe twice, but your ass done set a new world record," Pete said, shaking his head.

"But I ain't the only one who's doing it," Bambi said with tears in her eyes.

"You right," Pete said, wiping away Bambi's tears. "But you're the first one to get caught."

"Y'all gon' fire me?" Bambi asked, looking Pete directly in his eyes.

She was waiting for the axe to fall, and Pete smiled. He had Bambi right where he wanted her.

"I'm sure we can work something out," he said.

"Nigga, please… If you just wanted some free pussy all you had to do was ask," Bambi said, dropping the good-girl image.

"Bitch, I ain't trying to hear that shit. You just better have yo ass here after everybody leave tonight, or I will tell my sister to fire your ass," Pete said with a smirk.

"Cheap-ass-negro!" Bambi shouted after Pete walked out of the dressing room.

The rumors about Bambi had Pete overexcited. He couldn't wait for the night to end. Pete kept checking the time on his gold Movado watch. He was hoping the women wouldn't go too far past the three a.m. closing. Pete thought he was being discreet but he wasn't. Bambi, Victoria and Tameka all noticed his excited behavior. Tameka and Victoria immediately was wondering what was going on. Closing time finally arrived and Pete started shouting.

"Finish up! Closing time! Finish up!"

Tameka knew her brother well enough to know he was up to something. Instead of confronting Pete with her suspicions, Tameka decided to play the background. She didn't change her routine. They sat, counting money like they normally do, checking who made the most money that night. Pete paid O.J. and Boo Rock for their services. After Anna Marie was declared the big winner the women hit the showers. One by one they walked out the place. Except for Pete, Bambi, Tameka and Victoria, they were the last ones left. After he volunteered to close up on his own, Tameka slowly realized what Pete was up to. She agreed and walked out the club with Victoria.

Once Pete was satisfied that Tameka and Victoria were gone, he locked the doors to the club and headed to the showers. Bambi was standing in the middle shower butt naked with nothing but steam surrounding her. Pete was undressing and Bambi walked over to him. She whispered in his ear.

"Let me get that."

Bambi softly bit Pete on his ear before dropping to her knees and pulling Pete's boxers down. Pete's dick was semi-hard. Once Bambi started licking his balls, his dick jumped to full attention. Bambi began to slowly slip Pete's dick in and out of her warm mouth. She was about to pick up the pace when Tameka burst in.

"So this was the urgency?" Tameka asked with her hands on her hips.

Bambi jumped up, and Pete fumbled with his shorts, trying to think of something appropriate to say.

"Damn Tameka, can't you see I'm taking care of business."

"Business...?" Tameka asked, looking at Bambi's body. "I wouldn't call this business, big brother. I'd definitely say this is pleasure."

Tameka started walking toward the butt naked Bambi. Pete saw an ensuing problem and jumped in.

"Hold up, this me right here, sis," Pete said, cutting off Tameka's path. "I do think you need to go catch up with your girl, Victoria."

"Come on Pete," Tameka said, smiling. "We can share, can't we?"

Looking from Pete back to Tameka Bambi's eyes widened with surprise.

"Share...? This ain't no Jerry Springer shit."

"Me neither," Pete said, shaking his head. "You do know I'm your brother."

Tameka was clearly upset. She was seething when she turned to look at Pete then at Bambi. She stared at Pete.

"Nigga, we all grown here. I don't want to fuck you. I'm on the pussy just like you," Tameka said. Then she turned to Bambi again. "Either I'm going to get my pussy ate, or I'm going to eat some pussy. It's that simple."

Bambi was no stranger to eating pussy since she was bisexual. Although she would've enjoyed eating Tameka's pussy, Bambi reclined on her back, and decided to get her needs satisfied by a pro. Pete wasn't about to be left out.

"Fuck it!" he said, positioning himself over Bambi's head.

Tameka opened Bambi's legs and was shocked by Bambi's scent, especially since she had showered.

"This ain't gon' work," Tameka said, raising her head.

"What's wrong?" A frustrated Pete asked.

"Bambi, you gon' eat me out. Pete, you just hit that from behind,'"

Tameka said, pulling down her jogging pants.

"Why? What's wrong?" Bambi asked, sitting up.

Tameka was already pulling her black thong down and was standing naked from the waist down.

"Ain't nothing wrong, Bambi. I'm just so horny I need my pussy to be soothed right now."

"This way better anyway. Now y'all can get me on out the way and just do y'all," Pete said, sliding the Trojan over the head of his dick.

Watching Pete for a beat, Bambi nodded, standing. Tameka was on her back on a bench with her legs opened. Bambi moved to the edge of the bench. She bent over, giving Pete total access to her moistened pussy.

Bambi slid Tameka's shirt up and rubbed her hands up and down Tameka's taut stomach. She moaned softly from Bambi's touch. Smiling to herself, Bambi began kissing and sucking on Tameka's inner thighs. Inch by inch, Bambi made her way up to Tameka's love box. Tameka's breathing became shallow and the moaning grew louder. When Bambi finally ran her tongue on Tameka's clit, Tameka lost it.

"Oh yes, yes," Tameka sighed repeatedly, grabbing Bambi's blond hair. "Yep, lick this pussy."

Bambi stuck her tongue deep inside Tameka's pussy, snaking it around inside her walls. She simultaneously played with Tameka's clit. Then Bambi took Tameka's clit in her mouth, and started sucking on it.

Wrapping her logs around Bambi's neck, Tameka held Bambi's head on her pussy and became lost in the moment. Bambi worked her magic on Tameka's clit and wiggled her ass. Pete didn't need to be asked twice. Positioning himself behind Bambi, he ran his dick up and down her inviting opening.

Inch by inch Pete slowly put nine inches inside Bambi.

"Oh shit, hmm!" she sighed when Pete's manhood entered her.

Once he had all of himself inside of her he picked up the pace.

"Harder! Harder!" Bambi ordered, between licking Tameka's clit.

"Take that." Pete said, smacking Bambi on her ass.

Pete was stroking Bambi so fast and hard he kept making Bambi miss Tameka's clit. Bambi began to grunt.

"Slow down baby, slow down," she said in hopes of getting a rhythm that would benefit them all.

Pete slowed down and Bambi focused back on Tameka's quivering pussy. Bambi stuck her index finger inside of Tameka and ran circles around Tameka's clit with her tongue. Pete stopped smacking Bambi on the ass. He reached around and started massaging Bambi's clit.

"Hmm ah yes, ah yes," Bambi said huskily.

Tameka grabbed Bambi's blond mane and grunted, "Right there."

She climaxed. All her sexless nights had finally ended in one big blast. Tameka came long and hard.

"I'm coming! I'm coming!" Bambi managed from under Tameka's thighs.

"Oh shit! Me too," Pete said, fucking rapidly.

Pete and Bambi exploded at the same time. After Bambi climaxed she fell on top of Tameka. There was a scowl on her face.

"I gotta go shower," Tameka said, pushing Bambi off her. "And make sure you clean up too," she said, pointing to her brother.

"I am," Pete said, pulling the rubber off.

He shrugged, walked to the bathroom, pissed and flushed the toilet. Then he stood staring at his reflection in the mirror.

"My sister's a trip," he muttered.

*

Two weeks went by, and no one mentioned anything about that night. Bambi knew Tameka and Victoria were tight like a couple. She kept everything on the hush to avoid drama. Bambi wasn't worried about Victoria beating her up. It was Tameka's wrath that Bambi was worried about. Taking advantage of the situation by blackmailing Tameka, crossed Bambi's mind, but Tameka was too aggressive for Bambi's liking. Instead of trying to blackmail Tameka, Bambi got her to give one of her girls a job at the club. Tameka had Bambi set up an interview, and the two left it at that.

Bambi's friend's name was Barbie. High yellow and pigeon-toed, she was five-five, and weighed one hundred and thirty-eight pounds. Dyed blond hair, she wore deep blue contacts and used to call herself Barbie Doll. Tameka shortened it to Barbie. Tameka didn't want any of the strippers using names they had used in the past. In Barbie's case her stage name fitted and all Tameka could think of was being Ken.

CHAPTER FIVE

Ass By The Pound quickly became the official weekend spot. The club garnered the reputation of being a perfect place to go for enjoyment and fun. Tameka decided on the name of the club because that was how all the big spenders described it, Ass By The Pound. The place was on the tongues of all the heavyweight drug dealers in Gary, East Chicago, Hammond, Michigan City, Indiana, and even some parts of Illinois.

The club was doing so well three regular strip clubs were forced to close down shop. Ass By The Pound had stolen all their high paying customers. Two other clubs decided to compete by breaking various laws and regulations, including full nudity, and prostitution. They did all right until police found out, and set up an undercover sting inside the clubs capturing everything on video. When the clubs were closed, there was no other real competition. Ass By The Pound reigned supreme.

Barbie was a perfect fit. She was bold like Renee, and wild like all the other women. The crowd couldn't get enough of Barbie when she first started. She came in, and immediately started making a lot of money. Her run wasn't long. After three weeks her looks didn't fascinate the crowd anymore, and Barbie was forced to get creative. She was running around chasing every dollar she could.

Bambi played the background, and just did her job. She had learned she couldn't trust anybody from work. That meant both her coworkers and customers. Bambi warned her friend, Barbie to stay away from Tameka and Pete because they were "bad people."

"I won't mess with them two," Barbie said.

They decided to watch each other's back inside the club. Renee meanwhile, continued to be a private, but cool person. She never went out with Anna Marie, who was always hanging out, and they had never been to each other's houses. Renee remained a mystery to the other women, but because of her personality no one really cared.

Anna Marie was still playing mind games with the men. Using them for their worth then throwing them away, Anna Marie started making bets with Renee on how many gifts she would receive from each suitor. The bets spiced things up for Anna Marie and brought out a determination within her to excel.

Tameka and Victoria's relationship continued along with no changes. Everything appeared all right, but inside the privacy of their apartment, they remained estranged. Victoria focused on school and stacking her money while Tameka slowly started turning back into a party girl. Tameka couldn't get her needs met at home and went elsewhere to get it. She would hit the clubs in search of one-night stands. Although Victoria wouldn't let Tameka come near her, Tameka still wasn't giving up.

Midterms came and Victoria was exhausted. She had spent the past week studying for her exams. Now she was done. Victoria was walking out of her classroom, thinking about the money she missed by not dancing over the weekend. She had all the intentions of making up the money she missed out on. She planned on going straight home and resting. On her way out to the parking lot Victoria was met by a young, brown skinned woman. She stopped Victoria and spoke.

"Excuse me, your name's Victoria right?" she asked, staring at Victoria's tired eyes.

"Do I know you?" Victoria asked, squinting.

"Yeah girl, we in the same psychology class," the girl said, smacking her lips.

"Oh yeah," Victoria said, smiling at the girl, but really didn't remember her. "What can I do for you?" she asked.

"I heard you doing a little something on the side, and I'm trying to be down," the girl bluntly stated.

Victoria was caught off guard. She had tried to keep her personal life very guarded, especially at school.

"I'm not sure I know what you talking about," she smiled.

"C'mon Vee, you ain't gotta front for me. I'm trying to get paid myself."

"Paid how?" Victoria asked.

"Stripping…" the girl said with attitude. "What you thought?"

"Have you ever stripped before?" Victoria asked.

"No, but it can't be hard." The girl looked at Victoria with desperation in her eyes and said, "I need some extra money. My lights cut off and everything."

Victoria didn't want to hear a sob story, and was too tired to refuse. She pulled out a pen and a piece of paper and wrote down the address to the club. "Be here at seven o'clock Friday night."

The woman clutched the piece of paper in her hand like it was diamond.

"Thank you. I really do need this," she smiled gratefully.

"Don't worry about it. It's still on you to actually make the money. By the way, what's your name?"

"Tonya, Tonya Pierce," she said, still smiling and nodding.

"Alright Tonya, I'll see you Friday night," Victoria said, walking away.

Victoria turned around and saw the way Tonya's spirit seemed to be lifted. She secured the piece of paper in her pocket. "Friday night, I won't be late."

"Here," Victoria said and stuffed a wad of bills in Tonya's hand. "Get your lights on."

"Oh God, bless you Vee. One day I'll give it back. Thanks a lot thank you."

"Okay, you're welcome," Victoria said and walked away. "Fo real, that's a hyper girl right there," she said aloud, entering the parking lot.

Friday night came faster than Victoria expected. The late nights she stayed up studying for her midterm exams had really exhausted her. She slept a whole day and a half, and still felt tired. Victoria had planned on being in the club with the other women setting up for the night's show. Victoria looked at her watch and realized she forgot to tell anyone about Tonya's audition. She walked over to where Tameka was cleaning and said, "I forgot to tell you. This girl pulled up on me about joining us."

"What girl?" Tameka asked.

Victoria put down her cleaning rag, "This is the girl from my school."

Tameka stopped cleaning and looked directly in Victoria's eyes.

"You know I don't have a problem with other females dancing here. Shit, the more the merrier. What I will have a problem with is a little Miss know-it-all college girl, coming up in here thinking she better than us."

"Fo' real, Tonya ain't even like that," Victoria said, not knowing what Tonya was really like. "I ain't never interfered, but she's a good girl and she needs this chance. For me, let's give her a try."

Tameka wanted to say no, but couldn't. Victoria had a way of making her feel weak. They both knew it.

"All right, we'll give her a shot."

"Thank you," Victoria said, giving Tameka a hug then kissing her on the lips.

Tameka was caught off guard by Victoria's sudden act of affection.

"You're welcome," she smiled.

Seven p.m. Tonya walked in apologizing.

"I'm sorry I'm late Vee, it won't happen again. I had to drop my little sister off at our grandma's then grandma wanted me to take her to get her medicine, then…"

"Calm down Tonya," Victoria said, laughing. "You're not late, you right on time, see." Victoria said, pointing at a clock on the wall.

"Oh good," Tonya said, exhaling.

Tameka looked at Anna Marie then at Victoria. "What's up with this Vee shit?"

"Nothing baby," Victoria said walking to Tameka. "She don't mean a thing by it." Victoria gave Tameka a kiss on the lips and sat down.

"I know this bitch ain't playing me for soft. Like she got me whipped or something…" Tameka mumbled to herself.

Anna Marie looked Tonya up and down. "Quit trippin', girl. Can you dance?"

"Yeah, I can dance. I wouldn't be here if I couldn't," Tonya said with a attitude. "Why you ask me that?"

"Quit trippin', girl. You just don't strike me as the stripping type," Anna Marie said, shaking her head and laughing.

"I agree with Anna Marie," Tameka said, grabbing her keys. "We'll put you on next to last and have Renee close us out. That way she can know what to expect."

They all agreed, and the women then went to get a bite to eat. Back up in Ass By The Pound, the night started off slowly as usual. The women walked around the club accepting drinks, and mingling with the customers. This was their way of allowing any stragglers to see a full show and more importantly, the women didn't lose out on any money.

It wasn't until after midnight when the club actually got crunk. Tameka was the first performer to take the stage and do her thing. While Tameka had the crowd's full attention, the rest of the women started working the crowd for lap dances. Tonya did poorly. She received an 'A' for effort, but she had the rhythm of a rock n' roll white girl at a Rastafarian club.

Tameka continued to dance onstage, watching Tonya move from customer to customer, not getting one lap dance right. After Tameka finished her routine she went to find Victoria.

"Where did you get this wannabe from?" she asked Victoria.

"What's wrong?"

Victoria was surprised and Tameka shook her head.

"Your girl, Tonya, gon' ruin us. That's what's wrong."

"Calm down, baby. It can't be that bad."

"Oh yeah," Tameka said, turning Victoria so she could see Tonya attempts at giving a lap dance. "She got no rhythm. She can't dance!"

Victoria laughed at Tonya excitedly bouncing up and down on a customer's lap.

"Remember I couldn't give a lap dance at first either, but I knew how to dance. I'll tell you what," Victoria said, facing Tameka. "If she can't dance we just gon' have to jump on stage with her and improvise."

"I just hope we don't," Tameka said, sashaying away.

The night progressed. Tonya didn't get any better at giving lap dances. She actually thought she was good because the customers were paying her for two and three lap dances at one time. Any insecurities Tonya may have had at the beginning of the night had vanished by the time she hit the stage.

She was given the stage name, Peaches by Tameka because of her thick, curvy body. Tonya was eighteen years-old but looked about twenty-five. She wore her hair shoulder length. It was dyed honey brown to match her golden brown skin complexion. Tonya stood five-four and weighed one hundred and forty pounds. Her green eyes and her bowlegged stance were Tonya's best features. She wasn't lying when she said she needed the job. Tonya was raising her seven year old sister by herself on minimum wage, working at a fast food restaurant.

She waited for Boo Rock to announce her and Tonya prayed. She didn't want to mess up her routine. The last couple of days had been used for preparation. Now she was only a few nervous seconds away from performing it in front of a live audience. Boo Rock called her to the stage and Tonya ran on the stage and fell.

"Oh shit!" O.J. said, nearly splitting his sides laughing.

"Chill out, O.J.," Pete said, trying not to laugh too hard. "This is her first night."

Tonya quickly regained her composure and started her routine. She was attempting to grind to R. Kelly, *Seems like You're Ready*. Instead it looked like she was trying to break dance. The crowd began to laugh causing Tonya to stop her routine and stare at them with an open mouth. She turned to run and Tameka jumped on the stage stopping her. Tameka pulled Tonya to the middle of the stage and got behind her. She wrapped one of her arms around Tonya's waist and began to slow grind.

While Tonya was trying to find her rhythm, Victoria and Anna Marie were onstage working the poles. The crowd calmed down and money was soon being thrown onto the stage. After Tonya had enough and began to walk off the stage.

"Pick up your money," Victoria shouted to her.

Tonya was so overwhelmed by the women's generosity tears fell from her eyes as she collected her money. The women exited the stage and Renee closed the night out.

"I knew yo ass couldn't dance," Anna Marie said, counting her money. "Quit trippin', girl. You can barely walk."

"I'm sorry," Tonya said, looking at Tameka. "I guess I'm fired, huh?"

Tameka looked at Victoria then at Tonya before she spoke.

"Nah, you a'ight. We'll work with you," she said.

"Or make you a waitress," Anna Marie said, laughing.

Victoria looked at Tonya and wrapped her arm around Anna Marie's neck.

"Fo real, get used to the jokes because we family around here."

Tonya nodded her head as the women started telling jokes about Barbie. Saturday night didn't belong to the women. It belonged to Pete. Since opening day Pete had been supplying the customers with weed but this Saturday night the customers only wanted to get high. Pete couldn't believe how fast the weed went. He was forced to deal with a weed supplier out of New York. Pete sold Hydro, but was unable to reach his main supplier in Texas. He took a chance on the New York connect just to get by, and the Purple Haze shit was a hit. He sold all of the stash he brought to the club within two hours. Pete was forced to go home, and get some more because the Haze was in popular demand.

The customers weren't the only ones buying Purple Haze, the dancers were too. Tameka, Anna Marie, Barbie and Bambi each bought sacks for themselves. They were able to stash their weed because the customers were smoking blunts with them.

Renee didn't smoke weed and was cool. Victoria wanted to smoke some weed, but couldn't because of Tameka. Victoria still wouldn't let her guard down around Tameka. Tonya wanted to smoke, but Victoria wouldn't let her. Victoria took a liking to Tonya and determined to look out for her well being.

The night finally ended and the women couldn't wait to leave the club. Tameka sent Victoria on her way, telling her she would see her later. Anna Marie, Bambi and Renee had already left. Victoria gave Tonya a ride home. Tameka let Pete leave early because he had a date. Boo Rock and O.J. left after she paid them. Tameka was left all alone with Barbie and planned to take full advantage of the situation.

"What's up Barbie?" Tameka asked, sitting down on a bench.

"What's up girl?" Barbie said, putting on her thong.

"You," Tameka replied, lecherously eyeing Barbie.

"I know that's right," Barbie said, laughing. "What's up with you, Tameka?"

"You," Tameka said, standing. "You what's up. We grown folks and we the only two here, I'm trying to see you, Barbie."

Barbie was still way too high and stared in disbelief at Tameka. She had a half smile on her face when she said, "Tameka girl, stop playing."

"I ain't playing," Tameka said, walking up to Barbie.

She tried to tongue kiss her, but Barbie pulled away.

"Hold up. Ain't you with Victoria?"

"Look we're two consenting adults. We grown. My relationship with Victoria ain't got nothing to do with here and now. This right here is about you and me, Barbie," Tameka smiled.

Tameka pulled Barbie close to her, and attempted to kiss her again. This time Barbie didn't resist. She embraced Tameka. Tameka stuck her hand inside Barbie's thong.

"Oh, that feels so good," Barbie moaned softly.

"Lay on your back." Tameka said, massaging her pussy lips.

Barbie did like she was ordered. She started taking off her clothes. Tameka planned to take her time with Barbie and got butt naked. Tameka pulled Barbie's thong down and kissed her right above her clit.

"Whew!" Tameka said, jumping up. "You a little too strong down there for me... Ah, why don't we just switch positions and I'll owe you one."

Barbie was beyond embarrassed, but she switched positions anyway. Furiously she tried not to let Tameka see her reaction. Tameka was on her back while Barbie got on top of her and started tongue kissing her. Barbie slid her hand down to Tameka's breasts, massaging, first the right breast then the left. Working her mouth down to Tameka's breast, she slowly kissed and sucked Tameka's right nipple. Then she moved her tongue around in a circular motion. Barbie did the same thing to Tameka's left breast while slipping her hand between Tameka's legs.

"Hmm, that's what I'm talkin 'bout. Show mama what you got," Tameka moaned.

Barbie ran her tongue up and down Tameka's toned stomach. Sliding her index finger inside of Tameka's throbbing pussy, Barbie began finger-fucking her. Tameka inhaled deeply when Barbie added a second digit to her hot box. Slowly, Barbie worked her two fingers in and out of Tameka's gushy pussy while sucking Tameka's soft breast. Tameka was now sloppy wet and Barbie pulled her fingers out and smelled them. Tameka smiled because she knew you could bottle her scent. Barbie stuck her fingers in her mouth and twirled them around, causing Tameka's smile to widen.

"Hmm..." Barbie smiled. "Tasty."

Barbie lowered her head and slowly licked Tameka's outer lips. Tameka sighed when she felt Barbie's fingers opening her pussy up and burying her tongue deep inside of her. Tameka grabbed Barbie's head and rode her tongue like it was a joy stick. Barbie eased her tongue up to Tameka's clit, flicking it. Sliding one of her fingers back inside Tameka's pussy, she sucked

Tameka's clit. Barbie pulled her finger out of Tameka's pussy and eased it down to Tameka's asshole. Tameka screamed when Barbie's fingers forced its way inside her tight asshole. Barbie smiled and bit Tameka's clit.

"Ooh yeah, that's what I'm talkin bout. Give it to me!" Tameka screamed.

Barbie rammed her finger in and out of Tameka's asshole while she sucked Tameka's hardened clit. Grabbing Barbie tightly by the head, Tameka held it over her pussy. Barbie continued to invade her brown-wrinkle. A minute later, Tameka was exploding like a minefield.

"Oh shit! Oh God…!" she screamed and continued to hold Barbie's head down wiping her cum in Barbie's mouth.

When Tameka finally released Barbie's head, Barbie raised her head. Tameka smiled when she saw some of her cum smeared across Barbie's chin.

"How was it?" Barbie asked, letting it drip down her breasts.

"Hmm, all right," Tameka said, getting up to take a shower. "I'll give you a call back."

Barbie waited until Tameka turned on the shower before she said, "Stuck up bitch!"

Sunday night came and things were back to normal. The customers still bought some Purple Haze from Pete, but they smoked it moderately. During sets Tameka pulled Pete to the side.

"Don't fuck with that bitch, Barbie, raw."

"What you talking about?" Pete asked, laughing.

"Pete, we grown, you know what I'm talking about," Tameka said in a forceful tone. "Your dick's gon' get your ass in some shit the clinic can't fix!"

"Where is this coming from?" Pete asked.

Tameka looked around then back at Pete before she spoke.

"I was about to give that nasty bitch some head, but when I stuck my head down there, her cootchie smelled like death, my brother."

"I see where you coming from, and 'ppreciate the heads up. That's what sisters are for," Pete said, nodding his head.

"Without question, my brother…"

CHAPTER SIX

Victoria loved the money she made from stripping, but hated the acts she had to do to get the money. She had been stripping for six months, and had saved up a nice amount of money. Victoria felt it was time for her to put the stripper act to rest. Tameka and the rest of the girls had to be informed about her decision. Victoria approached her when they were getting ready to go to their jobs at the Baby Food Center.

"Did you sleep well?" Victoria asked.

Tameka stared at Victoria for a beat. Victoria's question was out of the ordinary. She probably wanted something, Tameka thought.

"I slept alright. How about you?" she asked.

"I couldn't sleep at all. I had a lot of thoughts running through my head," Victoria said, sighing.

She was trying to bait Tameka in. Victoria sighed heavily. It was early in the morning, but it wasn't early enough. Tameka knew exactly what Victoria was doing. She decided to play along.

"What kind of thoughts?"

"A little of this… A little of that… But mainly about stripping," Victoria said, looking at Tameka.

Tameka's ears perked up. Her curiosity was piqued. She leaned over to her roommate, very interested.

"What about stripping?" she asked.

Victoria took a deep breath and said, "I want to quit stripping."

"What?" Tameka shouted in surprise.

"You gotta be kidding me, Victoria. We just now starting to get a team of dancers and you want to quit. Why?"

"Fo' real, because I'm tired," Victoria said flatly.

"Tired of what?"

"Tired of shaking my ass in front of men to get a dollar… I'm tired of feeling disgusted with myself every time I do it. Fo' real, I'm just sick and tired of being soo damn tired."

Silently, Tameka shook her head. She stared at the frustrations on Victoria's face. It made her look older than she was. Tameka thought about it before she spoke.

"We grown folks here, you must be confused. We don't take our clothes off for dollars. Twenties, fifties, hundreds, yeah… Dollars, no," she said.

"Fo' real, you don't ever get tired of stripping in front of men? People you say you despise…?"

"Hell no!" Tameka exclaimed. "I don't despise men. Shit, I love men… Jackson, Grant, Franklin. You must be sick, that's all."

"I ain't sick," Victoria shot back. "I'm just tired of stripping, and I want out."

Tameka chuckled. "You just confused right now."

"I ain't confused!" Victoria shouted.

"You gotta be if you talkin' 'bout givin' this easy money up," Tameka said, walking closer to Victoria. "If you need another weekend off… Cool. I need you Victoria. Anna Marie and Tonya need you too. All I'm saying is that you think about what you're going to do before you do it."

"Alright, but don't expect much. I ain't you," Victoria said, nodding her head.

"And what's that supposed to mean?" Tameka asked, taking offense to Victoria's statement.

"Fo' real... I didn't mean nothing."

Tameka inched closer to Victoria and said, "Nah, it must mean something. What did you mean?"

"All I meant was you've changed. It seems like all you care about is stripping," Victoria said with a sigh, shaking her head.

"That's not true and you know it," Tameka said, wrapping her arms around Victoria. "I care about you more than anything," she added, kissing Victoria. "Just think about it. Now let's go before we be late."

"I will," Victoria said, grabbing her purse before they left.

All day long her mind kept drifting back to the conversation she had with Victoria. Tameka couldn't concentrate at work. She was really worried about Victoria quitting. Tameka enlisted Anna Marie and Tonya in getting Victoria to stay on. Anna Marie told Victoria what Tameka wanted her to say, but winked and whispered, "Do what you think is best." Anna Marie wanted Victoria to be happy, no matter what that meant.

Tonya on the other hand completely undermined what Tameka wanted her to do. Tonya admired Tameka, but had love for Victoria. Victoria was the one who gave her the chance to make some money. Even though Tonya couldn't dance, Victoria was the one always helping and encouraging her. Victoria never gave up on her. Tonya loved her even more for building a personal relationship.

She would stop by Tonya's apartment on a regular basis with gifts of clothes and toys for Tonya's little sister. Tonya thought about everything Victoria had done for her. She called Victoria and expressed her displeasure with Tameka's pressure-tactics.

"If you want to quit, then you should. I'll miss you, but I want you to follow your heart," Tonya explained, sounding emotional. "I'll ask Tameka for advice whenever I get stuck. And if she doesn't know I'll ask Anna Marie."

The conversation left Victoria thinking. She ultimately stayed because of Tonya. Victoria didn't want to leave Tonya around the big, bad wolf all by herself. Victoria feared Tameka would turn Tonya out. Victoria knew Tameka and wasn't about to allow a beautiful, young, and naïve Tonya get taken advantage of.

Tonya and Anna Marie were happy Victoria decided to stay, but it was Tameka who was the happiest. Tameka knew as long as she kept Victoria around stripping, there was a chance she would be able to turn her all the way out.

New Year's '01 was less than two weeks away. Tameka wanted to throw a New Year's Eve bash for all the customers. She said it would be a way of giving back to the ones that made them successful. The entire staff had a meeting in the club to discuss the event.

"Quit trippin', girl," Anna Marie said and sat her glass of Hennessy down. "You want us to dance for free?"

"C'mon, we grown folks here, girl. They gon' pay," Tameka said, smacking her lips.

"Now I'm confused," Renee said. "You said we giving back to those who made us successful. So if we're giving something back…" Renee paused to make sure she was making sense. "Then it's free for them."

Tameka looked around the club at all the women dancers but her eyes stopped on Victoria.

"Something's going to be free but it won't be us. There will be no cover charge and drinks will be free. A little something to show our appreciation, that's all."

"What about O.J. and Boo Rock? If there's no cover charge and no fee for drinks, how're they going to get paid?" Barbie said, looking at O.J. She had developed a crush on the bartender.

"We gon' have to pay them out of what we make?" Tonya asked.

"That's right, college girl," Tameka said, smiling. "We gon' all put in. We can afford to take a loss for one night. And Tonya, if your grades reflect your true smarts you know we gon' make sure you're taken care of."

Victoria shot Tameka an evil look. She had mentioned that she would surprise Tonya with a thousand dollars if she made the Dean's list. Now that Tameka was putting it out in the open, Victoria was going to really put it out there.

"Yeah Tonya, we were going to surprise you, but Tameka's going to match whatever I give you. Ain't that right baby?"

Tameka smirked. "Yeah boo, that's right. One thousand dollars each..."

"No twenty-five hundred each," Victoria said with a smile.

Tameka wiped the smirk off her face. "Twenty-five hundred... Now back to New Year's Eve. Y'all with it?"

Everyone agreed and the group went into preparation mode for the night's entertainment. When night fell, the club was packed. The women were used to the club being packed, what they weren't used to were all the small-time hustlers trying to tip them dollars. Bambi, Barbie and Renee adjusted quickly. The three performed in clubs where anything above a dollar meant they had to do something extra. To them, a dollar was a dollar and that's how they carried it.

Tameka and Anna Marie on the other hand, took offense to being tipped one dollar. Victoria couldn't believe how high and mighty the two thought they were. Instead of confronting them Victoria grabbed a paper bag. She told them to put the dollars in the bag if they didn't want them. Anna Marie quickly threw the dollars she made inside the bag and walked off. Tameka was a little more hesitant to part with her money, but she was riding with Anna Marie and threw her dollar bills inside the bag.

"What are you going to do with the bunch of ones?" Tameka asked.

"I'm going to put them in the bank, so please, keep 'em coming," Victoria said, smiling.

Anna Marie was walking by Tonya when a man grabbed her.

"Excuse me," she said, snatching her arms away. "You don't know me like that. In fact, you don't know me at all."

"Damn," the man said, flashing Anna Marie his thousand watt smile. "That's what I'm trying to do if you give me a chance."

The look of disdain on her face said that Anna Marie wasn't remotely attracted to the rough looking man.

"You couldn't afford a minute of my time," she said, pointing at the one dollar bills he was holding. "Quit trippin' and step your game up. I'm high maintenance."

"Damn slim, it's like that," the man said and stood to his feet. "You shouldn't judge a book by its cover."

"Quit trippin', I'm also judging by the pages," Anna Marie said, pointing to the man's entourage.

The man looked around the table and seen all his guys holding a handful of one dollar bills. The man let out a laugh.

"You got that. But I'm still trying to get at you. My name's J.T," he said, extending his hand.

Anna Marie liked his resiliency but J.T. sill didn't have the paper she liked. Despite her better judgment she shook his hand. "Pocahontas," she smiled.

"How beautiful, this is a dream. I've dreamed about you all my life," J.T. said, smiling.

"Cute but corny," Anna Marie said, laughing. She looked around the club and then said. "Well, you've already cost me about three hundred dollars. So I'll see you around."

"No doubt," J.T. said, watching Anna Marie's behind.

Anna Marie made it to the other side of the club and someone grabbed again. She spun around ready to give the person a piece of her mind, but the sight of the man's jewelry stopped her short.

"Hey baby," she said with a soft smile.

The man returned the smile, showing Anna Marie a mouth full of platinum.

"My name's Shawn. I'm only in town for a couple days and I'm spending them taking care of business. My nights will be for you to take care of me."

Anna Marie could see Shawn was about his business. There was ice dripping from his ears, neck, and wrists. Despite the obvious signs of money, she still had to clue him to what time it was.

"Can you afford me?" she asked.

Shawn pulled out a stack of hundred dollar bills, and put them on the table.

"What you think?"

"That's a start," Anna Marie said, trying her best not to show too much excitement.

"All right mami. Why don't you pick up the dough and let's bounce," Shawn laughed.

"Quit trippin', player, I ain't finished working."

She saw Shawn pulling out another stack of hundred dollar bills and looked at her face. He waited a beat before speaking.

"You are now," he said dropping the money on the table.

Anna Marie looked around before she snatched up the money.

"I'll be back in twenty minutes."

Shawn and Anna Marie were leaving the club and Pete stopped them.

"I need to talk to you for a minute," he said to Anna Marie. The two walked away from Shawn then Pete continued. "I see you ain't got no shame."

"Fuck you, nigga! What do you want?" Anna Marie said, smacking her lips.

Pete pulled out ten one hundred dollars bills and said, "For you."

Anna Marie didn't accept the money. Shaking her head, she said, "Nigga, you trippin. What's that for?"

"In your dreams, bitch! I wouldn't pay for that rundown shit." Pete paused and looked at Shawn. "But I guess there's plenty of suckers out there for you, huh?" Pete laughed.

"So who is the money from?"

Pete put the money in her hand. "J.T," he said, walking away.

She left with Shawn, and Anna Marie didn't even know where they had driven to, until Shawn turned off the 2000 Cadillac Escalade rental truck. Shawn took Anna Marie to the Syberis. She had been there plenty of times, but didn't complain. Anna Marie couldn't get J.T. off her mind. He seemed broke to her, but now she had her doubts. She tried to put J.T. out of her mind, and focused on Shawn.

As soon as Shawn and Anna Marie were in their room Shawn closed the door and attacked Anna Marie. Anna Marie was caught off guard because normally the men had a little more self-control. He was kissing Anna Marie so roughly, he bit her lip.

"Hold up. Quit trippin', man," she said, pushing him away. "There's no rush. We got all night."

"I ain't with no teasing," Shawn said, already halfway taking off all his clothes. "I had enough of that in the club."

"All right let's go," Anna Marie said, when she saw the length of Shawn's dick.

Picking up Anna Marie, he threw her on the bed. She could tell that Shawn was in a barbaric mode and Anna Marie removed her panties. Anna Marie didn't want him ripping it off her. Shawn was already in the midst of slipping on a condom.

He got on top of Anna Marie and began kissing her. Sliding one of his fingers inside Anna Marie's pussy, he worked it in and out of her. Shawn played with Anna Marie's pussy for about thirty seconds. He quickly flipped her over and pulled her onto all fours.

"What the…" Anna Marie started, but Shawn had roughly shoved all ten inches of his manhood inside of her. "Ooh shit!" she screamed.

Shawn was pumping her pussy. Withdrawing slowly, he rammed his dick deep inside Anna Marie's sappy love box with all his might. He kept stroking her long and hard for a while. Then Shawn started smacking Anna Marie on her rotating ass.

"Who's yo daddy?" he shouted.

Anna Marie realized she was in some crazy shit. Shawn was plowing his dick in her so forcefully that Anna Marie's head kept banging against the headboard.

"Quit trippin' and slow down, nigga!" she shouted angrily.

"Shut up and take this dick," Shawn shot back.

The whole ordeal lasted about two minutes and forty seconds. Anna Marie's body felt like it was five hours and with five different guys at once.

"Damn! Quit trippin', nigga. I heard about trying to kill the pussy but your ass took it to a whole 'nother level."

"I had to get my money's worth," Shawn said, between breaths. "That shit was sure nuff good too."

"I hope it was," Anna Marie said, already planning her escape.

Laying her head on Shawn's hairy stomach, Anna Marie rubbed his chest until he was asleep. She made sure Shawn was sound asleep then Anna Marie called Victoria to come get her.

Victoria pulled up in front of the room and Anna Marie ran out the room leaving the door wide open.

"Drive," she ordered, jumping into the car and slamming the door quickly.

"What's up, girl?" Victoria asked.

"That nigga trippin, he car-razy!"

"Fo' real…?"

CHAPTER SEVEN

Anna Marie ended up losing money that weekend. Shawn paid Anna Marie well, ten thousand dollars to be exact, but Anna Marie didn't know if it was worth walking around with his hand prints engraved on her ass for a week. After she left the Syberis, Anna Marie decided to call Tameka.

"I'm taking the next two nights off," she said.

"Why…" Tameka asked.

"Just in case Shawn's crazy ass shows up again," she added and ended the call.

The holidays came and the women had Christmas dinner at Tameka and Victoria's apartment. All of the women bought at least one gift for each other, but Tonya received the most gifts. Victoria worked with her, but Tonya still didn't have any rhythm. Her tips came in small numbers and the other dancers knew it. They all picked a household accessory to give her. Victoria went all out, buying Tonya a brand new living room set with a forty-two inch screen television. She also used the one dollar bills to open a bank account for Alisa, Tonya's little sister. It already contained three thousand dollars.

The women had a very lovely Christmas and when it was over, they directed their focus on the New Year's Eve bash. Victoria and Anna Marie concentrated on decorations while Tameka dealt with the beverages. Tameka wasn't concerned with buying the expensive bottles that were normally sold at the bar. Since patrons would be drinking for free, she focused on the better bargain. Tameka did splurge on a dozen cases of Moet. They would be able to bring in the New Year on a half way decent note.

New Year's Eve had arrived and Ass By The Pound was jumping. The place was jam packed. It would have been all good if half the customers weren't petty drug dealers. The increase in their clientele disturbed Anna Marie because she couldn't stand broke-ass-niggas. Anna Marie put her displeasures aside and decided to enjoy the night.

The whole crowd was enjoying themselves. Tameka was entertaining some women while Victoria was chatting with some of the regular patrons. Bambi was busy giving lap dances and Barbie was doing her thing on stage. Renee was having a drink with Boo Rock. Some of the petty drug dealers flocked Tonya. The night was going according to plan. Guests were happy and thought they were getting something for free. The women were still making their money.

"Excuse me miss, may I have this dance," a man whispered in Anna Marie's ear.

When Anna Marie turned around, she was blinded by an iced out lion symbol dangling from a platinum chain.

"Don't I know you?" she asked, smiling.

"Oh, it's like that. We have a little conversation, and you forget a brother," the man grinned.

Anna Marie knew the man's face and tried desperately to place it.

"I think I know you."

"Maybe this will help," the man said, reaching into his pocket and pulling out a knot of dollar bills. "Remember me now...?"

Anna Marie laughed. "J.T.," she said and gave him a hug.

"Oh, it's all love now," he smiled, hugging her back.

Anna Marie stepped back and looked at every inch of his six-two frame.

Dark as night, J.T's skin wrapped his one hundred and eighty-five pound, muscular body tightly. His light brown eyes sparkled with his smile. His jet-black hair had deep ocean waves. J.T.'s facial hairs were evenly trimmed into a neat goatee. Wearing a powder blue and white Sean John jumpsuit with some throwback Carolina blue and white Jordan's, J.T. was fresh. His left ear, neck and wrist were all iced out.

"Hmm, I see you clean up well."

"You think," he said, smiling.

J.T. handed Anna Marie a gift wrapped box and her smile widened.

"What's this?" she asked, ripping the box open.

Her eyes lit up and she burped when she saw the shiny diamond bracelet with earrings to match.

"Just my late Christmas present," J.T. said. His winning smile was on full display. "Something small..."

"Thank you," Anna Marie gushed happily.

The courting came to an abrupt end when one of the small-time drug dealers threw a bottle of Moet at Tonya. She was on stage going through her routine.

"Nigga, what's your problem?" Renee asked angrily.

"The bitch can't dance and neither can you," the man shouted and stood up.

Tameka and Victoria rushed to aid Tonya while Renee stood her ground.

"Nigga, you's a bitch! A broke-ass bitch at that!"

Pete couldn't get there fast enough. Before Renee realized, she was sprawled out across another customer's table.

"Who's the bitch now, bitch?"

"You are," Pete said, breaking one of the chairs across the young man's back. "Get your ass outta here," Pete ordered and began stomping the man.

"Aw, hell naw!" one of the young man's friends said.

He jumped up and caught Pete with a two-piece to the face. Pete staggered, but before he could throw a punch O.J. hit the dude in the back of the head with a Moet bottle. Before the man could hit the ground Boo Rock caught him, and slammed him on top of the guy who had hit Renee. Pete, O.J. and Boo Rock stomped both of the guys out while the crowd watched.

The New Year's Eve bash made Pete go back to being selective about who he let inside the club. He thought the next generation of hustlers would be laid back like the veterans in the game. He was mistaken. Pete still wanted to build their clientele and hit the streets in search of more big-spenders.

Pete's search paid off because the first two weekends in January the club was filled with people with money. He even found an all-female clique getting major paper called Cash Money Queens to stop in. Not only did the ladies show, but they spent a lot of money as well. Three of the young ladies even became customers. Ass By The Pound was definitely making a statement in '01. Tameka was trying to lead the way.

Tameka called a mandatory meeting to discuss the future of Ass By The Pound. She wanted everyone in attendance because her plan would affect all of them. Everyone was there except Tonya. She wasn't seeing any major money and Tameka started the meeting without her. Tameka sat her Smirnoff Ice down, and began to speak.

"I know y'all all wondering why I called this meeting, but it's simple."

"Money..." Anna Marie said, smiling.

"That's right, money," Tameka said, nodding. "We all grown folks here and I know that's what we all want. That's why we here every weekend to get it."

"I'm sorry I'm late," Tonya was said, rushing to find a seat. "Grams was trippin' on watching Alisa."

"It's cool," Tameka said. She took a couple sips of her beverage. "Like I was saying, we grown folks and money, we all need it and we all want it. Pete has given us a chance to get it at an even faster pace. We now have a higher quality clientele."

"I'm not following," a confused Bambi said.

"It's simple," Tameka said, surveying the entire room. "We strip more days."

"Oh, hell no," Anna Marie said, jumping to her feet. "Quit trippin', girl.

Three nights a week is enough."

"Fo' real, Tameka," Victoria said in a soft voice. "Let's not forget we do have day jobs too. Plus, Tonya and I have school."

"Fuck our day jobs," Tameka said, pounding the table. "That shit's chump change compared to what we making here."

"Chump change to y'all, but me and O.J. got good jobs," Boo Rock said, referring to their jobs in the steel mill.

"And I for one ain't about to give that up," O.J. said, sitting his drink down.

"I can respect that," Tameka said, nodding her head in O.J. and Boo Rock's direction. "On the days y'all two don't feel like doing nothing, we'll find replacements."

"I ain't feelin it either, Tameka," Renee said.

"And why is that?" Tameka asked.

"Shit, because I be tired. Plus, I do have a personal life," Renee said, pausing and looking around the room. "I don't know about y'all, but my life don't revolve around this club."

"It pays the bills, don't it?" Tameka angrily asked.

Victoria stood up. "Fo' real, hold up, Tameka... Me and Anna Marie both said we weren't feelin' it either. Don't jump down Renee's throat for not being with it either."

"And let's not forget Me and Boo Rock ain't with it either," O.J. quickly added.

"I guess y'all wanna stay petty with this. Well, I ain't gon' stop y'all," Tameka said, shaking her head. She walked away with her head held unusually high. Pete got up and went after his sister.

"Fuck her! We doing this together. All those in favor of dancing more days raise your hands," Anna Marie said. Barbie was the only one who raised her hand. Anna Marie looked around the room and said. "It's settled. We keep it the same."

Pete ran outside and found Tameka in front of the club. She was crying.

"Hey what's this about?" he asked, wiping her tears. "We the Smith's, and we don't let lil' shit get to us."

"Them ungrateful bitches!" Tameka said, dabbing at her eyes. "I started this shit. It was my vision. If it wasn't for my foresight them backstabbing bitches wouldn't have shit!"

"I know. I know." Pete said rubbing his sister's back. "You know what you gotta do right?"

"What?"

"Find some more bitches that's going do as you say," he said, smiling. "Now straighten up and go find some more ho's 'cause them bitches in there is tired."

"You right, fuck 'em bitches. I'm out," Tameka said.

She smiled and hugged Pete tightly. Tameka walked to her car and drove off.

After Tameka's little meeting she had no love for her coworkers, including Victoria. Tameka went about her day barely speaking to Victoria. She even on a couple occasions went without saying anything at all to her. Tameka gave Anna Marie the same treatment. They were closest of friends and Tameka felt betrayed by them. Instead of reconciling their differences Tameka set out to replace her partners. She hit the strip club every night trying to find new women to put on her team. After all, the club was in her name, and she planned to use that to her full advantage.

Anna Marie wasn't the least bit disturbed by Tameka not speaking to her. She felt Tameka had changed for the worse since they started stripping, and knew it was only a matter of time before the two of them fell out. Anna Marie had two other people on her mind anyway, J.T. and Victoria.

Anna Marie and J.T. had become a real couple. J.T. had a certain quality about him that turned Anna Marie on. For the first time in her life, Anna Marie wasn't with a man for his money, she was with J.T. for his character.

She even found herself being totally honest with J.T. about her past. He didn't like it, but respected her for telling him. J.T. put both pasts to the side and concentrated on the present. That made Anna Marie happy, and wanted someone else to be that way also.

"What's up, girl?" Anna Marie said, walking into Tameka and Victoria's apartment. "Is Ms. Mean Bitch around?"

"No, she's out doing her own thing," Victoria laughed.

"Quit trippin', girl and tell me exactly what that mean," Anna Marie said.

"I have no idea," Victoria said, closing the door.

The two women sat down in the living rom. Anna Marie turned to Victoria.

"That's why I'm here. Are you happy? Quit trippin', and tell me if this living arrangement's working out."

Victoria stared at the bold eyes of Anna Marie and put on a fake smile.

"Fo' real, it's great. I know you might think we're having problems but we're not."

"Quit trippin', girl. This is me you're talking to. I know sump'n's wrong. I can see it in your eyes."

"I'm fine Miss Nosey. Fo' real, I really am."

"Then Victoria tell me why you been depressed, huh? Is it Tonya?"

"What do you mean is it Tonya? What exactly are you implying?" Victoria asked, confused.

Anna Marie started off stuttering. "I... I ah, just thought, I mean, I figured."

"You think I want to sleep with Tonya?" Victoria asked.

"Yes."

"Fo' real, Anna Marie, I can't believe you," Victoria said, jumping to her feet. "Fo' real, I ain't gay."

"Quit trippin', girl. I thought you and Tameka were lovers," Anna Marie said, looking baffled.

"One time!" Victoria shouted. "Fo' real, it only happened one time. I was drunk and she did me. And I've been ducking her ever since."

Anna Marie moved closer to console Victoria. She hugged her friend before speaking.

"That's terrible, baby. No wonder you been walking 'round all down and out. You need some dick, badly."

The two women laughed and Victoria said, "Fo' real, I don't know 'bout all that, but I'm cool. Tameka comes and goes as she pleases. I don't have to worry about her hittin' on me and Tonya is like my little sister. Fo' real, she looks up to me. This Tameka thing just has me all messed up. I don't know what I was thinking."

"Fo' real, girl, shut your mouth," Victoria said, nudging Anna Marie.

The two friends spent the rest of the evening playing catch up on each other's lives. Anna Marie talked about J.T. and Victoria told her about classes. It felt like old times and Anna Marie was relieved Victoria hadn't been completely turned out.

CHAPTER EIGHT

A month had gone by since the meeting. Not only was Tameka still not speaking to Victoria and Anna Marie, but she still hadn't found any other new strippers. Tameka refused to lower her standards even though she knew something had to give. She would find attractive females who knew no tricks or ugly women who knew all the tricks. The attractive women she courted, and slept with a few. The ugly women, she didn't bother wasting her time on.

Tameka decided to venture to the nearby Hammond. The city had three strip clubs and the third club is where Tameka found Porsha. She walked by Tameka's table, causing Tameka to spill her drink. Tameka prayed the natural beauty could dance half as good. When Porsha was called to the stage, Tameka left her table and sat at the edge of the stage. Porsha didn't disappoint, she had enough rhythm and tricks to hang with the girls. She was finished dancing, and Tameka called her over.

"What up, Ms. Thang?" Tameka asked, smiling.

"Beware of smiling faces because they always want something," Porsha said, refusing to sit down.

"And what do I want?" Tameka asked innocently.

"Lady, my time is money. So whatever it is that you got to say, just say it," Porsha said with a lot of attitude.

"Up-front, I like that. And you're right," Tameka said, going inside her pocket and pulling out a hundred dollar bill. "We grown, time is money."

"I can see you about business," Porsha said, taking the money and sitting down. "So, what's your business?"

"You," Tameka said, smiling. "I want you to come and dance with me."

"Dance with you where...?"

Tameka took a sip of her Hennessy before saying. "Ass By The Pound."

"I heard about that place. The word is they gets major paper and it's exclusive. How're you gonna get them to accept me? And why?"

Tameka leaned forward and said, "I am Ass By The Pound. I started it. It's my name and I can hire whoever I want. I'm looking to build my roster up and I'm choosing you. Are you with me or not?" Tameka asked, pausing long enough to let her words sink in.

She saw the smile appear on Porsha's face for the first time, showing her even, and white teeth.

"Hell yeah, I'm with you. When do I start?"

Tameka smacked the table and said, "That's what I'm talking about. You can start this weekend but there's a catch."

"I should've known there was a catch to it. What's the catch?" Porsha said, smacking her lips.

"Nothing major, we dance Friday, Saturday and Sunday night but I'm looking to add on two more nights. Will that be a problem?" Tameka said with a chuckle.

"Girl, that's all," Porsha said, waving her hand. "I thought you was about to say I had to sleep with some nigga or sump'n."

"No way, I ain't with that. I want all the pussy to myself," Tameka said, smiling.

Porsha returned the smile. She got the address from Tameka and sashayed away from the table.

+

Tameka had been trying to feel Renee out since they hired her. Tameka wanted to suck Renee's pussy ever since the first night when that customer ate her pussy. Renee had been with them the longest and managed to stay real private. She remained a mystery that Tameka wanted to solve. She didn't know Renee's likes or dislikes. The only thing Tameka knew about Renee was she liked to get her pussy eaten. Tameka caught Renee in the parking lot by herself.

"What's up, Renee?"

"Another day — another dollar," Renee said nonchalantly.

"I hear ya on that one. But I been meaning to ask you sump'n," Tameka said.

"Ask me what?" Renee asked, looking up.

"Are you gay?"

"I should've known yo skank ass was going to ask me that," Renee said, shaking her head.

"What you mean by that?" Tameka snapped her head back.

"Just because I don't say anything, doesn't mean I don't know anything."

"And what does that mean?" Tameka said, confused.

"It means this," Renee said, walking within two inches of Tameka's face. "I know you fucking these other sluts that work here, but I ain't the one. I ain't gay and I'm not trying to be gay."

"All right, damn," Tameka said, laughing. "We grown, take a chill. I don't know anything about you, and I was just trying to get to know you. That's all."

"Humph," Renee said, watching Victoria pulling into the parking lot. "Know me sexually is more like it. Don't ever come at me like that again, or I'll tell Victoria what I know," Renee said, angrily walking away and going inside the club.

The women were ten minutes away from opening up for the night and Pete walked in.

"This woman says she's here to dance," he said, pointing at Porsha.

"Oh yeah, she cool. I hired her, Pete," Tameka said, rushing forward.

"I wish y'all start giving me a heads up," Pete said, and walked back to the door.

"Everybody, this is Porsha, Purple Passion. Porsha, this is everybody," Tameka said, pointing to Porsha.

"What place is she gon' dance in?" Bambi asked.

"We gon' put her next to last, so she can see how we operate," Tameka said to Bambi. She turned to Porsha. "This ain't no regular strip club. We ain't got no rules so get your money by any means necessary."

The club was crowded as usual. Dancers were working the room like pros. Everybody was getting money, even Tonya. Finally catching on to the art of lap dancing, she was now getting money. Tonya's on-stage routine still needed a lot of work.

Porsha fitted right in. She worked the crowd while Tameka watched, smiling. The crowd was drawn to her new and beautiful face. Porsha received the attention Tameka was expecting. This only made the other women work that much harder, except Victoria.

She had found a regular patron, who never paid for a lap dance unless it was given by Victoria. He never spoke to any of the other women and had only asked Victoria her name. Victoria found the man's silence sexy, but weird. Her mystery man was six-one and weighed one hundred and ninety-five pounds. Light brown with matching eyes, his long braids dropped down pass his shoulders and he wore a neat, thin goatee. Victoria didn't even know the man's name, but knew he was a little older than she was.

Porsha worked the crowd and paid close attention to her coworkers when they went on stage. She wanted to have an idea of what her routine should be like. Porsha was formulating a routine in her head, but when Barbie let a male customer eat her out on stage in front of everyone, the routine she was planning went out the window. Victoria was the only one left to go ahead before Porsha, and her brain started working overtime.

With Victoria working the stage, Porsha spent time in the dressing room still brainstorming. She had her big shot image to uphold and wasn't about to let her inhibitions get in the way. She had already made more money in her first night than she would make in a week at a regular strip club. By the time Victoria finished her routine, Porsha had made her mind up.

"Gentleman and ladies," Boo Rock said, nodding to the Cash Money Queens. "I present to you the lovely Purple Passion."

Porsha hit the stage full of confidence. The entire audience had their eyes fixated on the beauty of Porsha's six foot, no heels, weighing one hundred and eighty pounds, 36D-25-42, Amazon-like physique. She was a brick-house with beautiful dark skin lit up by the gray contacts she wore. Her long micro mini braids, worn pinned back in a ponytail.

Seems Like You're Ready by R. Kelly got Porsha's routine off to a slow and sexy start. She used the entire song for stripping away her black thong set. The next song Porsha chose was Silk's, *Lose Control*. She engaged both of the sliding poles. Jodeci's *Fiendin'* found Porsha reaching into the audience and pulling a handsome, young man on the stage with her. She instructed him to bring his chair. The man sat in his chair in the middle of the stage with a huge grin on his face.

Porsha started off by giving the young man a lap dance while unbuttoning his Polo shirt. Raising the man's shirt up, Porsha kissed and licked his stomach up then down. She glanced back at the crowd, smiled and began unzipping the man's pants. The crowd cheered her on wildly. Porsha held up her fingers instructing them to come out their pocket. Money rained on stage from all directions. Porsha looked at the man and held out her hand. He quickly went into his pocket, and counted out five hundred dollars. Porsha shook her head. The man counted five hundred more. Porsha had the man angle his chair in order to give the audience a better view.

Kissing him on his forehead, she moved down to his eyes, his nose and lips. The man tried to slide his tongue in Porsha's mouth. She pulled away, shaking her head. Porsha slid her tongue down his chest, his stomach, finally pulling out his dick. To the raucous cheering from the crowd, Porsha slipped the man's dick inside her mouth and started bobbing. Up and down she went on the man's dick without shame. Up and down. Up and down.

Porsha's head was bobbing for a full two minutes before she had all eight inches of his penis in her mouth. Before exiting the stage, Porsha walked over to Boo Rock. Grabbing the microphone, she said, "I'm sorry ya'll, but that's all he paid for."

Porsha walked past the man and blew him a kiss. He was sitting in the chair, holding his dick and looking dumb.

"You wild, girl," Tonya said after they had closed. "I ain't got the heart to let a nigga eat me out on stage. I damn sure ain't about to suck a nigga in front of nobody."

"Fo' real, that took a lot of guts," Anna Marie said, looking around at everyone. "It looks like you're going to fit right in."

"Sure does," Tameka said, smiling. "Hmm, hmm, it sure does."

Saturday night brought another problem in the form of a six-six, two hundred and sixty pound gorilla. The man was sitting in his chair when Victoria walked by on her way to dance for her mystery man.

"I can't get a dance?" the man asked, stumbling and appearing drunk.

"Sure you can, but I've got another customer waiting right now," Victoria smiled.

"Fuck that!" the man said, getting up. "You gon' give me that dance!" he ordered, reaching out for Victoria.

"Fo' real stop that and get away from me!" she yelled, smacking his hands.

Tameka witnessed the incident going on and ran to the bar. She grabbed a weapon and raced away.

"No Tameka!" O.J. shouted.

Running over to where Victoria and the man were arguing, and without saying anything, Tameka sliced the man across his back with a box cutter.

"How you like that? You wanna take something, huh? Take this," she said, slicing the man again in the back.

The man turned around and saw who it was. He drew his arm back to swing, but Boo Rock caught him in the back with a chair. The man stumbled forward and Tameka sliced him across the face. The man reached out for

Tameka and O.J. broke a chair across the man's back. He fell to the ground. By the time Pete arrived, the man was out cold snoring. Tameka spit on the man and Pete stomped away.

"I knew I shouldn't have let yo big ass in here," Pete said with his boot stomping away.

"He trippin'. Girl, you all right?" Anna Maria asked Victoria.

"Yeah, I'm fine," she said, still shaken.

"What happened?" Anna Marie asked.

"Fo' real, I don't know. I was on my way to give a lap dance, and he just started buggin' for no reason," Victoria said, her voice trembling.

"Who was you about to give a lap dance to?" Anna Marie asked, smiling.

"Excuse me," Victoria said, returning the smile.

"Quit trippin', girl. I've been watching you, and that dude over there for about a month now."

"I don't even know him. He's just a customer," Victoria said, leaving her mouth wide open.

Anna Marie looked at the gentlemen again and seen J.T. talking to him. "You might not know who he is, but I'm definitely going to find out."

Victoria shook her head and said, "Anna Marie, girl. Leave it alone."

"Quit trippin', girl. I will find out who he is first," Anna Marie said, looking over at J.T.

"Man, how long you gon' play this game," J.T. said, watching Anna Marie. "Say something to the girl."

The man sipped his drink and turned to J.T. He said, "I will when the time is right."

"And when is that, never?" J.T. asked, laughing.

"Nah Mr. Funnyman, I'm going to approach her when I come back off my trip."

"Oh, let's see. That's in about two weeks, right?" J.T. asked.

"Yeah, that's it. Two weeks," the man said.

"Alright Big Ken, I'm a hold you to yo word. Two weeks," J.T. said, smiling.

"I got you. But while I'm gone I want you to look out for her," Big Ken smiled.

"Fo' sho'," J.T. answered, watching Anna Marie and Victoria at the same time.

CHAPTER NINE

Big Ken was true to his word. Once his business was finished he hit the highway and headed back to Gary. Big Ken's business took longer than he expected forcing him to show up at Ass By The Pound on Sunday night, instead of Friday night. He sat in the club waiting on Victoria to come over. Victoria moved from customer to customer heading in his direction.

Once she was standing in front of Big Ken, he smiled and said, "Damn, it took you long enough."

"I beg your pardon," Victoria said, putting her hands on her hips.

"You don't have to ever beg me for anything," Big Ken said, reaching out for her.

"I bet," Victoria said, smiling.

She was getting in position to straddle Big Ken and give him a lap dance when he stopped her.

"Hold on," Big Ken said, holding Victoria at her slim waist. "Let's talk first."

Victoria looked around the club. She could see that Tameka was busy giving the Cash Money Queens lap dances.

"Alright," she said, taking a seat across the table from Big Ken. "So what do you want to talk about?"

"You," Big Ken said with a smile.

"Me...? I'm kind of involved right now," Victoria said, blushing.

"But you not happy," Big Ken said, leaning forward unto the table. "I come in here every weekend and see you release a lot of pent up anger when you be dancing."

"Oh, my bad... I didn't know I was talking to a shrink," Victoria said sarcastically.

"Nah, it ain't even like that," Big Ken said and leaned back in his chair. "You're attractive, very attractive. I just want to get to know you. That's all."

"I bet, Mr."

"Oh my bad, Kenneth," he said, extending his hand.

"And you are?"

"Victoria," she said, smiling.

Anna Marie saw that Victoria and Kenneth were talking. She headed straight to where J.T. was sitting.

"What's up, baby?" Anna Marie said, straddling J.T. "How you doing?"

"Better now. What's up?" J.T. said, wrapping his arms around Anna Marie.

"Something gotta be wrong? I can't just wanna spend some time with my boo?" Anna Marie asked.

"Of course you can spend time with me. But I know you, so I know something's up."

"Dang, that's what I get for trying to chill with my man. You being all suspicious and shit," Anna Marie said, pushing J.T. softly in his chest.

"Honesty, remember?" J.T. said, shaking his head.

"Alright," Anna Marie said, pouting. "Who is that dude Victoria talking to?"

"Okay, I see what this is about."

"What?" Anna Marie said innocently. "I can't look out for my girl?"

"Trust me, she in good hands. That's my man Big Ken and..." J.T. said,

POWER OF THE

looking at Victoria and Kenneth talking.

"Big Ken, you mean, the balla?" Anna Marie interrupted.

"Nah, he ain't no balla," J.T. said, shaking his head. "My man been out the game for a minute now. He's officially retired."

"Quit trippin'. I heard he's one of the biggest drug dealers in the city," Anna Marie chuckled.

"Damn, Miss Nosy." J.T. said with a frown. "You sho' do know a lot for somebody who don't gossip."

"Gossiping is one thing, listening to it is something else," Anna Marie said in a matter-of fact tone.

"Anna Marie, If you gon' listen to gossip make sure you listen to the right shit because yo information is faulty."

"Calm down, baby." Anna Marie said, rubbing J.T.'s chest. "I'm not trying to start a fight. I'm just trying to look out for my girl. I'm sure you can understand that."

His mood had become lightened when J.T. spoke.

"Yeah, I can dig it. But I'm telling you, Big Ken done been out the game for a couple years now. He just up and gave me everything one day. Fucked me up because he ain't never asked me for anything." J.T. paused for a few seconds before continuing. "'Cept to watch after yo girl, when he was out of town," J.T. added.

Over at the table where Kenneth and Victoria sat talking, he put his drink down.

"I'm an entrepreneur," Kenneth said.

"You mean you're a drug dealer...?" Victoria asked in a disappointed tone.

"No, I mean I own a cellphone shop and a couple beauty salons. I'm also in the middle of starting a record label. That's why I haven't been here. I was out of town trying to sign these two groups outta Texas."

"I'm sorry," Victoria said with sincerity. "It's just that I look around and all I see is drug dealers. I'm sorry I was wrong to have put you in that category."

"It's cool," Kenneth said, smiling. "But now tell me a little about yourself."

Victoria and Kenneth spent a majority of the night getting to know each other while Anna Marie kept Tameka away from them. Anna Marie was never down with Victoria and the whole lesbian thing. Now that Victoria had a chance to have a relationship with a real man, Anna Marie was going to do everything she could to help make it happen. After they closed the club, Anna Marie took Victoria to the truck stop so they could talk.

"I see you didn't do much tonight," Anna Marie said, glancing at the menu.

"Girl, shut up," Victoria said blushing. "Fo' real, that's all we did was talk."

"Quit trippin', girl. I know. I know," Anna Marie said, smiling. "For now..."

The two women ate and Anna Marie kept trying to pry about what Victoria and Kenneth talked about. Having no luck, Anna Marie decided to talk about her favorite subject, money.

"Well at least he's paid."

"It's not all about money. But yes, he got a little something," Victoria said, shaking her head.

"Little sump'n my ass," Anna Marie said, pointing her fork at Victoria. "He was that nigga not too long ago."

"What you mean?" Victoria asked confused.

"He's P-A-I-D," Anna Marie said, spelling it out. "Big Ken was the biggest drug dealer in the city."

"Fo' real, Big Ken...?" Victoria mumbled then she looked at Anna Marie. "Are you sure?" she asked.

"Am I sure?" Anna Marie said with a mouthful of food. "Quit trippin', girl. J.T. said Big Ken put him on, so yes, I am definitely sure."

Victoria didn't want to hear anymore. She didn't ask any other questions, and let Anna Marie do all the talking. Victoria's mind was racing one hundred miles an hour, thinking about all the things Kenneth told her.

She sat at the table both hurt and pissed off. She thought Kenneth lied to her about selling drugs and if he lied about the drugs, Victoria assumed he lied about everything else. She was pissed off for allowing herself to trust, and believe him.

Victoria hated that she had to wait a whole week before she would be able to tell Kenneth the things that were on her mind. She had refused to take his number out of fear. Victoria couldn't take the chance of Tameka finding Kenneth's name and number. They had decided to wait until the upcoming weekend to talk again and now she couldn't wait.

The week went by fast but not fast enough for Victoria. Normally she was talkative and merry, but since her conversation with Anna Marie, Victoria had become cold and short with people, especially with Tameka.

Friday night had finally arrived and Victoria couldn't wait any longer to confront Kenneth. One by one Victoria watched the customers entering the club. She anxiously waited to see Kenneth's face. She was disappointed, but Victoria remained focused. The club had been open two hours, and no sign of Kenneth. Victoria didn't want to give Kenneth a chance to get comfortable when he walked in and sat at a table by herself. She continued to watch the front door. To hide what she was actually doing, Victoria told the others that she wasn't feeling well. The women gave her their sympathies and went about making their money.

At two o'clock in the morning Victoria was beyond pissed off. She had started drinking Alize at midnight to calm her down but the alcohol worsened her mind-state. She had given up on Kenneth showing. Victoria was about to get up from her table and a group of men walked into the club. Kenneth was one of them. Victoria stared at him walking toward her.

"Bitch, what the fuck is your problem?" one of the men who walked in said.

Every head in the club turned when another said, "I told you Donnie. That bitch been up in here tricking while you was locked up."

"Oh shit!" Renee said aloud, watching Donnie walk in her direction. "This nigga done got out early."

Donnie and four of his guys surrounded Renee. Stared at her and asked, "Where my little girl at?"

Renee's eyes were wide and she looked scared. Donnie towered over her standing six feet-five and weighing two hundred and thirty pounds.

"She's at my sisters," Renee nervously answered.

"Bitch, you ain't shit!" Donnie said, smacking Renee down. "I risk my life to provide for y'all, and you leave me for dead."

"I'm sorry. I'm so sorry," Renee cried out.

Pete stayed on the sidelines watching and hoping things didn't escalate. He had no plans to get involved in Renee's personal affairs, but when Donnie smacked Renee he ran over.

"Hold up, playa. You can save that shit for when you get home. Ain't gon' be none of that in here."

Donnie looked at Pete for a beat and said, "Nigga, fuck you! Get the fuck out my face! This here, don't concern you."

Pete chuckled as O.J. and Boo Rock made their way over.

"You right," Pete said, swinging and connecting with Donnie's jaw.

"Nigga, you done lost your mind," Donnie said, staggering.

Before anyone else could throw a punch Kenneth and J.T. were standing in the middle of the crowd.

"Hold up," Kenneth said, looking at Donnie. "Niggas in here to have a good time and you fuckin it up. If anyone of you niggas throw another punch then I'm a get involved and you know what that means."

"It means, I'm a get involved," J.T. said, smiling.

Donnie definitely had the size in his advantage since the smallest guy in his group was six-two, two hundred pounds but Donnie also knew Kenneth and J.T. weren't talking about fighting.

"It's cool Big Ken. I don't want no trouble J.T." Donnie said.

He had only been gone a year, but still knew who ran the streets.

"Good," J.T. said, looking at Donnie's whole crew. "Now why don't y'all get the fuck outta here before it won't be cool."

"And another thing," Kenneth said, helping Renee off the floor. "Don't put your hands on her. If I come in here and she tells me you hit her…" Kenneth paused and smiled, shaking his head. "Lights out!"

"Nah, we straight," Donnie said, inching his way out the door.

In a few minutes, everything was back to normal, J.T. walked over to Anna Marie and Kenneth walked over to Victoria.

"Fo' real, you're in deep shit," Victoria said before Kenneth could take a seat. "But how can I be mad at you after what you just did."

"Why am I in deep shit?" Kenneth asked, sitting down.

"For lying to me," Victoria slurred.

"You're drunk and you're confused," Kenneth said, shaking his head.

"No, I'm not," Victoria said, waving a finger. "You lied to me about what you do. You are a drug dealer," she blurted.

"No, I'm not," Kenneth said, leaning forward.

"Yes, you are," Victoria quickly responded.

Kenneth looked Victoria directly in the eyes and said, "Are you going to let me talk, or is your mind already made up?" He waited for Victoria to respond. She remained silent and he continued. "Good, I'm not a drug dealer. I am who I said I was. I own a wireless communication shop and a hair salon."

"Fo' real…? And what do you be doin' on the side to get real money?" Victoria asked.

"Alright," Kenneth said in a low voice. "You want me to say it? Here it go, I used to sell drugs."

"Used to my ass, you still do. You're J.T.'s boss," Victoria laughed.

"Don't let J.T. hear you say that, he will definitely be offended," Kenneth said, laughing.

"Fo' real, it's true. Anna Marie told me so."

Kenneth signaled for J.T. and Anna Marie to come over. When the two arrived Kenneth said, "I need y'all help with something. J.T. who is your boss?"

"I am my boss. I don't take orders. I give 'em," J.T. said with a frown on his face.

"Okay, and Anna Marie, do I sell drugs now or did I in the past?" Kenneth asked.

Anna Marie gave Victoria a mean look when she realized Victoria really liked Kenneth.

"Heifer, is that why you been pissed off all week? Quit trippin', girl. I said he used to sell drugs. He left J.T. everything."

Victoria said nothing. She sat staring at the table feeling embarrassment flooding her body. Kenneth looked at J.T. and Anna Marie then he said, "Thank y'all. I got it from here."

Victoria waited for J.T. and Anna Marie to walk away. Then she said, "I'm so sorry. I don't know why I overreacted."

"Because you like me," Kenneth said, smiling.

"Maybe, just a little," Victoria smiled back.

Kenneth and Victoria sat and talked until the club closed. Renee came over and thanked Kenneth for intervening earlier. Tameka saw Victoria and Kenneth talking, but Kenneth was a guy, and Tameka paid the two no mind. After Renee's altercation, Anna Marie took the rest of the night off and spent it talking to J.T.

CHAPTER TEN

Tameka was starting to get stressed out, not from the dancing but from feeling alone. Victoria and Anna Marie were her two best friends. She used to talk to them at anytime and would tell them everything. Since Tameka stopped speaking to the two women, she only talked with Pete. Tameka loved her brother, but there were still some things she wasn't comfortable telling him. Tameka decided to put her pride to the side and make up with her friends.

She was in her bedroom getting dressed when Anna Marie arrived.

"Quit trippin', girl. What's this all about?" Anna Marie asked Victoria, entering the apartment.

"Fo' real, your guess is as good as mine," Victoria said, closing the door.

"I hope she ain't gone try to convince us to dance more. I ain't with that shit," Anna Marie said, taking a seat on the couch.

"Fo' real, me neither," Victoria said, turning off the television. "Three nights is more than enough. It's like she's trying to be greedy."

"It isn't about being greedy," Tameka said, walking into the living room. "We grown now. It's about keeping the customers happy and us retiring early."

"It's like this Tameka, the customers come and spend like they do because we only dance three nights a week. Look at the regular strip clubs that be open six and seven days a week, they might have one or two good nights a week. You know why? Because niggas get burned out on seeing the same shit every day," Anna Marie said, looking at Tameka, who was shaking her head.

"I agree," Victoria said, looking at Tameka. "Fo' real, would you want to see the same bitches every day?"

"Y'all right. We grown, I see y'all point," Tameka said.

"About time heifer," Victoria said, smiling. "Fo' real, we could've been put this behind us."

"I know. It just seemed like y'all was against me. Like I couldn't count on my two best friends to back me up," Tameka said, hugging Victoria.

"Quit trippin', girl and shut your petty-ass up," Anna Marie said, standing. "That was some real petty shit not speaking to us over something so small. If you do that shit again I'm a kick your ass," Anna Marie said with a wink and a smile. "Nah, get your ass over here, and give me a hug."

"I sure did miss my girls," Tameka sighed.

Things were still going well for the women. Ass By The Pound was still the most talked about strip club in the city. With the buzz going hot about the club, one would think the women were still seeing major figures, but they weren't. The increase in the number of dancers, and money kept dwindling. There was one night when the big winner made only eight hundred dollars. The decline in figures weren't due to a lack of patrons. There was always a full house. The smaller figures had to with the customers wanting to see something new and different. Customer's voiced their opinion and their request was taken into consideration. The partners decided to start holding contests.

A wet T-shirt contest was the first one held. The event was a big time flop. It went so badly, the customers booed the women off the stage. The next contest the women held involved them wearing a diaper, and an audience member changing her. The crowd was a little more receptive to this idea. It was different and the audience member spanked Tonya a couple times. The contests loosened the crowd up and allowed the women to make a little more money.

"I see y'all trying to climb back on top," Kenneth said to Victoria as she gave him a lap dance. "These some wild ass contests y'all be having."

Victoria looked Kenneth in his eyes and said, "You ain't seen nothing yet. Next month we got some wild shit lined up for y'all."

"Oh yeah…?" Kenneth smiled. "I can't wait to see what y'all gon' do next."

"Fo' real, and that's all you gon' be doing is seeing."

"Hold up, wait a minute," Kenneth said, holding Victoria by the waist. "Are you going to be jealous if I participate?"

"No," Victoria said firmly. "Fo' real, your ass still better not participate."

"Why don't you have a seat?" Kenneth offered.

Victoria bounced up and down on Kenneth's lap. She said, "I already got one."

"It's hard for me to be serious when you got my dick all hard," Kenneth smiled.

"My bad," Victoria said, climbing off Kenneth's lap. "Fo' real, what's so important? I don't understand," Victoria said, looking confused.

"Me neither," Kenneth said, adjusting his dick. "You say that you can only be my friend because you involved with someone else, but he can't be making you happy."

"And why is that?" Victoria asked.

"You and I both know I'm the one who arouses you," Kenneth said, leaning forward.

"Fo' real, don't let Tameka hear you say that."

"Tameka…?" Kenneth asked, stunned.

"Yes, Tameka," Victoria said, smiling. "Fo' real, she's supposed to be my significant other."

Kenneth sighed loudly and calmly leaned back in his chair. He stared at her with a deliberate look in his face.

"I'm not moved and I still want to take this friendship beyond this club," he said.

"What do you mean beyond this club?" Victoria asked.

"I want us to date. I want to take you out, wine and dine you. I want us to be able to talk without these distractions. I just want to spend more time with you because these weekends just ain't getting it."

Victoria leaned back in her chair and grabbed Kenneth's drink.

"What the hell?" she said before turning up his glass of Hennessy.

She drank every last drop. After a month of weekend meetings only, the two finally exchanged phone numbers. Their date was set to take place Wednesday and Kenneth couldn't wait.

Victoria was a nineteen year old hottie, who had never been on a date. Victoria was used to group settings, where she could blend in with the crowd, and avoid the focus being solely on her. Nervous couldn't even begin to describe the way Victoria felt. This was going to be her first real date. She not only didn't know what to expect, but how to act. To ease her fears Victoria went to a pro.

"Quit trippin', girl. You ain't got nothing to be nervous about," Anna Marie said, sitting in her car. The hard part is already done. Big Ken is open, girl."

"Kenneth," Victoria said, looking at Anna Marie. "Big Ken is long gone."

"My bad," Anna Marie said, smiling. "That's right. Stand up for your man then."

"He's not my man. We just friends," Victoria said proudly.

"Quit trippin', girl. You my girl and I know we been through this before. You not Tameka. You not gay. It's alright for you to like a man and Big Ken…" Anna Marie paused. "My bad, Kenneth, is not a bad choice."

"Fo' real, I know I guess I'm just scared. This is my first real date."

"Yes and no," Anna Marie said, turning in her seat. "This is your first official date but y'all been dating every weekend now. This will be no different. The only thing's a change of scenery."

"Fo' real, you right, girl. Tomorrow will be just another weekend date. Thanks. I got it from here," Victoria said, nodding her head and smiling.

"Quit trippin', girl. That's what I'm here for. Now don't be a hoochie-mama, and give it up on the first date," Anna Marie said, giving Victoria a hug.

Victoria laughed at the thought. "Shut up hooker. Fo' real, I ain't you," she said getting out of Anna Marie's car.

Victoria walked back into the apartment she shared with Tameka, and got ready for bed.

That night, Victoria tossed and turned in her sleep. The same illusions she had been having for as long as she could remember revisited. It made her rest very uneasy. This time her dream was so real it turned into a nightmare. It had been over a year since the dream had recurred. Victoria was beginning to think she had overcome it, but here it was all over again haunting her, causing her to stir in her bed.

The dream always started off the same way. A six or seven year old Victoria, lying asleep in bed and awakened by a man rubbing her leg. She cannot see the man's face, but something familiar about the man was frightening to her.

"What's wrong?" a sleepy-eyed Victoria asked.

The man rubbing Victoria's leg answered, "Nothing. I just wanted to talk to you. Can I talk to you?"

"Yes," the young Victoria answered.

The man continued to rub Victoria's leg, each time his hand inching a little closer up her leg.

"You know I've been watching you and you've been a good girl. Since you've been so good, I have something for you."

The man took his free hand and stuck it in his pants pocket pulling out a rainbow lollypop. "For you," he said, handing it to her.

"Thank you," Victoria said, taking the sucker.

The man's hand finally reached Victoria's panties. Victoria squirmed when she felt the man's finger outside her opening.

"Everything's going to be all right," the man said, prying one of his fingers inside her small opening.

"No-o-o..!" Victoria screamed, jerking up in her bed.

The loud sound awoke Tameka, and she came running into Victoria's room carrying her box cutter in her hand.

"What's up? Where they at...?"

"Huh? Oh, it was just a bad dream," Victoria said. She was soaked with perspiration.

"Damn girl! You scared me," Tameka said, closing the blade back inside the case. "I thought you got past all those bad dreams."

"Me too," Victoria said, getting out of her bed. "But I guess I didn't."

"You need me to sleep with you to make you comfortable," Tameka asked with sincerity.

"Nah, I'm all right. I just need to take a quick shower, and get out of these wet clothes," Victoria said, grabbing another nightgown.

"All right," Tameka said, walking back to her room.

Victoria gathered up her underclothes and headed to the bathroom. She stayed awake the rest of the night, trying to figure out what caused the nightmare to come back. The only thing she could think of was her date with Kenneth.

Victoria sat in her Ford Taurus listening to R Kelly's *TP2.com* CD. She listened to the song, *Fiesta* while she waited for Kenneth to arrive. She contemplated leaving several times but her curiosity wouldn't let her go. Victoria tried the lesbian thing once and it felt good during the act, but the feelings she had afterwards were not good. She wanted to try the straight route, to see how she would feel. Kenneth pulled up and Victoria got out of her car.

"I'm glad you made it," Kenneth greeted her with a smile.

"I'd never pass up the chance to see a good movie," Victoria said.

"And I thought you came because of my smile," Kenneth said, escorting Victoria to the ticket booth. Kenneth paid for two tickets to see *The Brothers* and they went inside. The two stopped at the concession stand and left with their hands filled with junk food.

"I'm glad to see that you also have a sweet tooth," Victoria said, bumping Kenneth with her booty.

Kenneth picked up all the candy, Victoria grabbed popcorn.

"You need to watch that thing before you break something," he laughed.

"This little old thing…?" Victoria said, smacking her butt.

Victoria's booty was far from little and the two laughed. They went inside and watched the movie. When the movie had ended, they got into Kenneth's 2000 Escalade and went to get some real food. Kenneth took Victoria to a soul food restaurant in Gary's midtown area. The couple was enjoying their meal and Victoria looked up.

"This is some serious food. I haven't eaten like this in a long time," she said.

"Yeah, the food here is real good. I'll tell the cook you like it," Kenneth said, setting his fork down.

"Fo' real, you know the cook?" Victoria asked.

"She's a childhood friend of mine."

"She…?" Victoria said, frowning. Kenneth laughed and Victoria asked, "What's so funny?"

"You," Kenneth said, wiping his mouth with a napkin. "For you to be in a relationship with Tameka, and for us to be friends you sho' do get jealous a lot."

"I'm not jealous," Victoria said defiantly. "I'm curious. Who is she?"

"First, you have to learn to keep your emotions in check. You're letting me know how much you really like me. Second, Toni is the cook. We grew up next door to each other. When I started getting money, I wasn't trying to keep it to myself. I helped those that were close to me, and Toni wanted her own restaurant. So I looked out."

"I bet she looked out too," Victoria said sarcastically.

Kenneth laughed and shouted, "Toni!" A large, dark skinned woman came from the back of the restaurant. "Toni, this is Victoria. Victoria, this is Toni."

Victoria was once again embarrassed, but asked, "How do you do?" Victoria shook Toni's hand.

Toni had to weigh every bit of two hundred and fifty pounds while standing only five-seven.

"I'm fine. And I can already tell you are if Kenneth's bringing you here to meet me," she said.

"Excuse me," Victoria said.

"I've known Kenneth my whole life. He has never introduced any female to the family," Toni smiled.

"Family...?" Victoria echoed, confused. "Fo' real, y'all related?"

"Not by blood," Toni said, putting her hands on Kenneth's shoulder. "We just look out for each other like we family. You're lucky. This here is a good man."

"Alright, all right," Kenneth said, blushing. "Enough girl talk, I'll talk to you later, Toni."

Toni kissed Kenneth on his cheek, bade goodbye and walked away. Once Toni was out of their sight Kenneth faced Victoria.

"Happy?" he asked.

"Of course I am," Victoria smiled. "Now I'm not the only one sitting here embarrassed."

The two laughed and continued talking while eating. It was after midnight and Victoria decided to head home. Kenneth took her back to her car where the two hugged and Kenneth kissed her on the forehead. Victoria smiled on the outside but was disappointed on the inside because she was looking forward to kissing Kenneth goodnight. Kenneth watched Victoria get in her car and leave. For the next two days, she couldn't keep her mind off Kenneth.

Friday and Saturday nights came and went so fast it was as if they never happened. If it wasn't for the money some of the women wouldn't have believed the nights came. A few of the women were living their lives only for the weekends. At the top of that list was Porsha.

She was money hungry and Tameka knew it. Tameka fell back and let Porsha get accustomed to making thousands instead of hundreds. Fucking Porsha was also part of the plan. She had wanted that the very first time she laid eyes on her. Tonight would be that night. Tameka had already arranged everything. She told Porsha to stay back and help her clean up. She had Pete leaving after he paid O.J. and Boo Rock. Tameka even brought in her goody bag.

When the club was closed, Tameka and Porsha were cleaning up. Porsha was in the middle of wiping off a table.

"I don't see why you picked me to help you. Why you didn't pick Victoria?"

Tameka didn't say anything. Instead, she went in the dressing room, returning with her goody bag.

"This is why," she said pulling out a nine inch strap on dildo.

"You gotta be kidding!" Porsha said, her eyes growing to the size of golf balls.

"Does this look like I'm kidding?" Tameka asked and started removing her clothes. "If you want to stay employed here get yo ass up on that stage and strip. Don't act like you ain't with it."

Wide-eyed and surprised, it took Porsha all of five seconds to weigh her options. Porsha got on stage and stripped. Once Porsha was naked, Tameka joined her on stage with two dildos. The nine inch strapped on, she carried a regular six inch one.

"What now, big man?" Porsha asked angrily.

"Lie on your back so I can give you a treat," Tameka lecherously smiled.

Porsha did as ordered. Tameka sat her dildos down and climbed on top of Porsha. Tameka wasted no time in thrusting her tongue deep inside of Porsha's mouth. The two kissed passionately. Tameka ran her finger nails up and down Porsha's upper body. Tameka started sliding her body up and down on top of Porsha's body. Tameka's hot body was grinding slowly. Soon she was rubbing her pussy hard against Porsha's body. Tameka was on fire and it was spreading. She broke their kiss, and licked her way down to Porsha's throbbing pussy. Tameka avoided the foreplay because she wanted to taste Porsha badly.

"Please God, let her be fresh," Tameka mumbled under her breath before she stuck her face between Porsha's legs. It smelled fresh and she went tongue first inside of Porsha's hot box.

"Oh... Yeah," Porsha said, squeezing her breasts.

Tameka kept licking away at the inside of Porsha's pussy. Her tongue circled Porsha's clit. Tameka grabbed the six inch dildo, sliding three inches inside of Porsha.

"Ooh, hmm..." Porsha gasped.

Sliding the dildo in and out of Porsha, Tameka sucked hard on Porsha's clit. Her body began grinding and bumping against Tameka's mouth and the dildo.

"Oh yes, yes, I'm... Ah." Porsha screamed, exploding.

She grabbed Tameka's head, pushing it into her pussy. Tameka didn't lose a beat. She kept licking at Porsha's clit until Porsha came with a force unlike anything Tameka ever seen.

"Damn, it's been that long," Tameka laughed.

"It's been a while since I've got it this good," Porsha breathlessly whispered.

"Well, it's not over yet," Tameka said, strapping on the nine inch dildo. "Come on, I want to hit that from the back."

Porsha rolled over on all fours. "Please, be gentle," she throatily whispered, waving her big ass in Tameka's smiling face.

Tameka eased behind Porsha, plunging all nine inches deep inside her. Porsha leapt forward, but Tameka caught her by the waist.

"Uh, uh, where are you going? You gon' take this dick," Tameka said, pulling out and ramming the dildo inside of Porsh'a pussy. It took Porsha a minute to get used to what Tameka was doing. Once she figured it out, she prepared herself to meet every big thrust.

Tameka was enjoying herself. She was smacking Porsha's big, round ass and forcefully stroking the pussy with her dildo. Porsha was a veteran and had an orgasmic thrill. After she was finished, Tameka was breathing hard, staring at a delighted Porsha.

"Next time I plan to be on the receiving end. So get ready."

Porsha nodded her head, smiling on her way to the shower. Tameka watched her fat ass disappear before bending over to pick up her toys.

CHAPTER ELEVEN

March '01 finally arrived. This was the month Tameka planned to bring Ass By The Pound back to its original glory. She had sat back and thought of different contests she knew the customers would love. It took a lot of persuasions on her part but she had finally talked Bambi, Barbie and Porsha into going all out for the team. While Tameka did have Porsha participating in the contests, secretly she didn't want Porsha involved. The two were still creeping on the weekends.

The second weekend in March caught all the customers by surprise. Bambi, Barbie and Porsha walked on the stage as Tameka grabbed the microphone.

"What's up ballas, shot-callas..." she announced, taking position in front of the three dancers. "Tonight's contest is the first of many of its kind. That is..." Tameka paused and smiled. "If you're willing to spend 'em ends."

The customers in the crowd started showboating. They were pulling out knots of money, letting it rain and saying, "Is this enough? We got that money to blow..."

Tameka smiled at the customers' response. It was better than she hoped for.

"I'm glad to see we ain't got no petty ass broke niggas in here."

The crowd shouted louder. Tameka knew a man's ego was his downfall.

"How much y'all willing to pay to eat these fine ass bitches pretty little pussies?"

"One thousand…" A customer immediately shouted.

"Fifteen hundred…" Another quipped.

Tameka nodded her head.

"Alright… All right, I see we got a couple big spenders up in here, but c'mon big ballas, the ultimate prize is a date with the girl of your choice."

"Two G's…!" A customer quickly shouted.

"Twenty two hundred!" another countered.

Tameka looked at the women on the stage. The bid exceeded three thousand, and was still going. Finally bidding maxed out at thirty-three, thirty-four fifty and thirty-five hundred dollars. Tameka was hoping for more, but was satisfied. The three customers were called onto the stage and Tameka gave them their instructions.

The first one to make their woman climax was the winner. It was that simple. The customer who paid thirty-five got to choose who he wanted to eat out. He chose Porsha. The customer paying thirty-four fifty was Princess from the Cash Money Queens, and she chose Bambi. The third customer was left to eat Barbie's pussy. Tameka gave the three customers the signal, and they began eating pussies.

Each customer used a different technique. The man eating Porsha out was licking and sucking on her clit, moving two of his fingers in and out of Porsha slowly. Barbie was the victim to the tongue of an amateur. Not only was he trying to spell the A, B, C's on her clit, but he was actually calling them out while he was doing it. Barbie thought about guiding the youngster in the right direction, but decided to let him suffer for now, and pull him up on the side. Princess was definitely stealing the show.

Princess decided not to follow the gentlemen lead by diving head first into the pussy. Instead, she started at the top kissing Bambi while she played with Bambi's titties. Bambi was going through the motions at first trying not to be aroused, but when Princess stuck her hand between Bambi's legs Bambi gave in. Princess started massaging Bambi's clit.

"Hmm, ah…" Bambi moaned loudly.

The crowd was already cheering wildly, but when Tameka walked over and stuck the microphone in Bambi's face, the crowd erupted when they heard Bambi moaning. Princess eased her way down to Bambi's breast, stomach, and finally to Bambi's pussy. Princess rubbed Bambi's stomach, working her tongue in, out and around Bambi's pussy. Licking her clit, she finished Bambi off three minutes later. Princess was the winner. The crowd was cheering, Tameka raised Princess's arm in victory.

"So which one of these lovely ladies do you want to take out?" Tameka asked.

"No sweetheart, I don't want one of them. I want you," Princess said.

Tameka was thinking about refusing, but the crowd started chanting encouragingly.

"Diamond… Diamond… Diamond…"

"All right, me it is," Tameka said, looking around and smiling.

"Quit trippin', girl. That's what her ass gets," Anna Marie laughed.

"What you mean?" J.T. asked.

Anna Marie wrapped her arms around J.T.'s neck and said, "Oh nothing. She talked them three stupid asses into degrading themselves and was trying to stay out the way. I'm just glad Princess chose her conniving-ass."

"I thought y'all was cool," J.T. said, rubbing Anna Marie's back. "Sounds to me like y'all got beef or sump'n…"

"Quit trippin', J.T. We ain't beefin. I just don't agree with some of the shit she be doing." Anna Marie said with a sigh.

"I know what you mean."

On the other side of the club Victoria was giving Kenneth a lap dance.

"I see you weren't even joking about that shit. Y'all contests getting better."

Victoria suddenly stopped moving and stared at Kenneth. She asked,

"You wanted to be up there eating one of them out or something?"

"When are you going to start giving me some credit? I'm not a dog in any kind of a way." Kenneth said, shaking his head.

Victoria started wiggling her butt in Kenneth's lap and said, "I'll start giving you some credit when you're able to control this monster up under me."

"That's not fair for two reasons. One, you're causing me to be aroused. I don't get aroused by none of these other women or the things they do. Two, when it comes to you I'll never be able to control any of my bodily functions," Kenneth laughed.

"I hear you talking," Victoria said, continuing to grind her ass into Kenneth's lap.

Tameka was proud of herself for making an extra thousand dollars at the expense of her coworkers. The only problem she had was getting ready for a date she didn't want. Tameka would have been satisfied going out with any Cash Money Queens member except Princess. Princess was just too manly for Tameka's liking. Tameka liked her women looking feminine not all masculine. Likes aside, Tameka stood in front of her full-length mirror, checking herself one last time before she went to meet Princess at the club.

Tameka was out of the club and going on her date. Victoria decided to spend even more time with Kenneth. She and Kenneth had been on three dates and the two still had not shared their first kiss. Always the gentleman, Kenneth never rushed Victoria into anything.

Victoria first thought Kenneth's patience and understanding were sweet, but her body was craving his affection. Victoria was ready to throw caution to the wind, and make the first move.

Tameka was trying her best not to have a good time with Princess, but it was hard. Princess wasn't the stud Tameka thought she was. Princess actually turned out to be cool. When the two left the club, Princess took Tameka to see the Chicago Bulls play Detroit Pistons. Both Tameka and Princess had a lot of fun rooting for the Bulls beating the Pistons in overtime. Princess took Tameka to the Navy Pier restaurant after the game.

"I liked you from the first time I saw you," Princess said, setting her wine glass down. "But you always intimidated me," she added.

"What?" Tameka asked in surprise. "I had you pegged as this kick-ass butch."

"That's how I had you pegged. I have to put on a tough front to keep niggas off me. I can't be looking soft in the business I'm in. You know what I mean?" Princess laughed.

"Yeah, I guess so," Tameka said, nodding her head. "I'm glad you picked me because you're actually cool people."

"Does that mean we can hang out more often?" Princess asked.

"That depends," Tameka said, sounding serious. "If all you want to do is chill. We can do that. If you trying to taste the kit-kat then the answer is no," she raised her brow and added.

"We're on the same page, so it should be no secret that I'm trying to do something with you. If not tonight, then another night," Princess said, looking Tameka directly in the eyes.

"Definitely not tonight," Tameka said quickly. "My bitch knows I'm with you."

"Another night then… We'll leave it at that and enjoy the rest of the night," Princess smiled.

Meanwhile, Victoria and Kenneth were still in their own world at the club. Victoria hit the stage second so she could enjoy the rest of the night with Kenneth. Victoria was in the middle of giving Kenneth a lap dance when she stopped and kissed him on the lips.

Her kiss caught him by surprise. He opened his mouth up to speak and Victoria stopped him by shoving her tongue deep into his mouth. They sat at their table kissing each other while customers and dancers both watched in shock.

POWER OF THE

Anna Marie walked by the table. "Quit trippin', girl. Go girl, but watch out for Pete."

"Fo' real, thanks girl," Victoria said, pulling away. When Anna Marie walked off Victoria looked at Kenneth. "Who's the man?" she asked with a smile.

"You the man," Kenneth laughed.

The weekend was over and everyone enjoyed it. The work week on the other hand brought problems for Tameka. One big ass problem, in the form of Princess, determined to get intimate with Tameka. She called Tameka seven times a day leaving sexual voicemails on her cellphone. Tameka answered her phone a couple times, begging Princess to chill with the stalker routine. It was to no avail. Princess continued calling. Tameka decided to wait until the weekend to confront Princess face-to-face.

Friday night came around, and it was business as usual. It was a rough night, Tameka showed up at the club with an attitude forcing the other women to do their job and stay out of her way. Victoria wanted to spend the whole night at the table with Kenneth, but couldn't. She didn't want to hear Tameka's mouth, and spend time actually working the crowd.

A little after midnight, Princess and her crew came walking through the club doors. Tameka was in the middle of giving a lap dance. Princess walked by her and Tameka grabbed Princess by the arm.

"Come on, we need to talk."

Princess' girls looked at Tameka like she was crazy. Two of the women started to step to Tameka, but Princess held up her hand and stopped them.

"Nah, everything straight," she said before walking off with Tameka. Once they were by themselves, Princess asked, "What the fuck is your problem?"

"What the fuck is my problem? Bitch, what the fuck is your problem?" Tameka asked with her hand in Princess' face.

"Get your damn hand out my face. Girl, you done lost you mind"

"Nah nigga, you the one that lost they mind," Tameka said in a nasty tone. "You stalking me and shit. Bitch, you don't know me like that."

"And you definitely don't know me like that. The way you disrespecting me," Princess said, walking toward Tameka. "Bitch, don't you know I can have your ass dealt with."

"First off, let's not forget who my brother is. Second, you's a peon. Yeah, you getting a little money but Pete will deal with you and your whole crew. And you know it. We grown folks here, so what we gonna do is leave this shit right here. You forget my number and I won't go tell right now. Deal…?" Tameka smiled.

Princess turned her nose up. "Deal," she said.

Tameka walked back into the club area. She misunderstood what a customer demanded.

"Excuse me, what did you just say?" she asked.

"Damn, sweetie why you all up in my convo like that?" The man asked, looking at Tameka.

"Because you talkin 'bout my woman," Tameka deadpanned.

"Like I said, Candy's Big Ken girl," the man said, laughing.

"Who the fuck is Big Ken…?" Tameka asked.

"That's Big Ken right there," the man said, pointing at Kenneth.

Tameka laughed and said, "That trick ass nigga ain't got a chance. Candy's my bitch. She's my pussy, so dream on niggas."

Tameka walked off and remembered seeing Victoria and Kenneth together. The vision played on her mind. "That bitch been playing me," she muttered to herself, heading toward where Kenneth was sitting.

"Can I help you with something?" Kenneth asked when she was on top of him.

"Yeah," Tameka said, sizing him up. "The word is out that you fucking Candy." Kenneth glanced at her and laughed. "So are you?" Tameka asked getting angry.

"I wish," Kenneth said honestly. "I just get lap dances from her."

"I'm just here to tell you to wish on, nigga. Candy's my bitch. She do what I say, when I say it."

"Fo' real, who the fuck you think you talking about?" Victoria asked angrily. "Bitch, you don't run me or my pussy. And don't be disrespecting me in front of the customers, especially my customers."

Tameka stared at Victoria unable to speak. She was stunned at how quickly Victoria had put her in check. She had been noticing little changes in Victoria's attitude but never did she count on Victoria checking her in public.

Kenneth sat at his table clapping his hands, laughing at Tameka.

"Shut your square ass up!" Tameka said, walking off embarrassed.

Victoria didn't want to make Tameka more jealous and walked away from Kenneth's table. Before disappearing into the dressing room, Victoria turned, winked and smiled.

Saturday proved to be a better night for everyone, especially the customers. This was the night Tameka was going to reveal her biggest contest. She was so sure this contest would be big, that she guaranteed three thousand dollars to each woman who participated. The thought of making an extra three grand appealed to all the dancers, but not all of the women wanted to participate. Bambi, Barbie and Porsha were the willing participants.

Tameka dressed in all red, grabbed the microphone from Boo Rock, and walked on the stage.

"All right fellas and ladies," Tameka said, turning her head to acknowledge the Cash Money Queens. "This is the night all of you've been waiting for—dreaming of even. Ass By The Pound proudly presents the first ever dick-sucking contest."

The crowd went crazy. "Aw nigga, that's me," one customer shouted, pulling out a wad of money.

"Nah nigga, I'm a be the one on that stage!" Another responded.

Tameka heard some of the patrons discussing spending big money and a smile clung to her lips. Tameka learned from the pussy eating contest not to let the customers watch for free.

"Come on now, this gon' be soo good, everybody gotta pay to see this one. I want all of y'all to reach in y'all pockets and let it rain money on this stage. C'mon lemme break out the umbrella."

Tameka produced a red umbrella and smiled when she saw the showering of dollars. Victoria watched Kenneth walk to the stage and throw five hundred dollars at Tameka's feet. Kenneth couldn't help but to laugh, walking away. J.T. was the next customer to throw some money on the stage.

"Come on… Where my big ballas at…?" J.T. said, turning to the crowd. "Other muthafuckas support y'all hustle, support the ladies hustle."

One by one the customer started throwing twenties, fifties and hundreds on the stage. Pretty soon it was raining in Ass By The Pound.

"That's what I'm talking about," Tameka said enthusiastically. "This shit is better than a porno because it could be you."

The customers finally stopped throwing money and Tameka motioned for the ladies to come on the stage. One by one Bambi, Barbie and Porsha walked on stage. Bambi and Porsha were blowing kisses to the excited crowd. Barbie turned around and shook her ass. Starting with Porsha, Tameka was going to make the crowd bid on the dancers, one at time.

Porsha was no stranger to giving head in front of a crowd. Her first night at the club she chose to solidify her spot by sucking a customer's dick in front of everybody. Since that night Porsha used the trick three times, and that was because the crowd was being stingy with the tips. She really needed the money. Each time Porsha sucked long enough to give the crowd a display of her oral skills. Teasing the willing customer, she wouldn't do it long enough for the customer to explode in her mouth.

For three thousand dollars Porsha vowed to give the customers a show like no other. Tameka started the bidding and an up and coming balla named Big Heavy won Porsha's luscious lips for the price of twenty-five hundred. Barbie was the next dancer auctioned off, the bids stopped at the low sum of twelve hundred dollars. Tameka knew the crowd was getting tired of Barbie's act and attitude, but until someone better came along she would continue to exploit Barbie for everything.

She saved Bambi for last because she knew niggas were going to reach deep into their pockets for the white, trailer-park trash. Bambi had been laying low for months, but Tameka hoped the slut reputation Bambi had built when she first started at the club was still being talked about. She opened the bidding up and quickly realized Bambi was still in popular demand. An old associate of Kenneth's named Vincent won Bambi's services for the amount of forty-seven hundred.

The three customers were seated on the stage Vincent turned to Bambi and said, "For forty-seven hundred you better master the art of sucking dick like that bitch, Vanessa Del Rio."

"As long as you ain't packin like Mini-Me, we gon' be straight," Bambi said with attitude.

"Trust me, sweetheart. If my shit was little I wouldn't be up here. I'm not into embarrassing myself like that," Vincent chuckled.

"Alright, King Cobra let me see what you working with," Bambi smiled.

Vincent pulled down his pants to reveal a skinny soft two inch dick. Bambi laughed.

"We'll see who's going to be laughing in a minute," Vincent said.

Tameka was still standing in the middle of the stage. She waited for the customers to be seated before she spoke.

"All right y'all the rules of the contest are simple. The women will suck these handsome men off until they cream. The ladies can use whatever tricks they know to make these men cum. That means they can jack you off a little, bite you, stick they finger up yo ass. Ha, ha, get freaky. We all grown folks."

"Ain't gon' be none of that, though," Big Heavy shouted, shaking his head. "I ain't with none o' that ol' freaky shit"

"All right, pops," Tameka said, laughing. "Let the contest begin."

Porsha wasted no time in getting Big Heavy hard. Cupping his balls in one hand and using the other to put his limp dick in her mouth. Within seconds, Porsh's mouth was filled with the meaty, seven inches of Big Heavy's dick.

Barbie didn't have to worry about getting her buyer hard. The young man pulled his boxers down, already semi-hard. By the time Tameka started the contest, he was fully hard. Barbie wrapped her mouth around the young man's extra fat six inch penis. She quickly learned his thickness was going to be a problem.

Bambi was curious to see exactly how large Vincent's dick will grow. While Big Heavy and the other young man chose to get their dicks sucked sitting down, Vincent was standing up and turned to the side so the audience could see Bambi swallow every inch of him. Bambi took Vincent's two inch penis in her mouth and started massaging his balls with her other hand. Twenty seconds later Vincent had a huge grin on his face. His dick stood fully erect at eight and a half inches. Bambi looked at Vincent and smiled before grabbing him by his bare ass pulling him deeper into her mouth.

Barbie was having difficulties keeping her mouth around the young man's thick shaft. She looked to her left and saw Porsha licking Big Heavy's dick up and down. Porsha would lick Big Heavy's dick up, down and then back up again. Then she took all seven inches of his rod into her warm mouth.

"Ah shit!" Big Heavy groaned.

Porsha knew it was only a matter to seconds and increased the intensity of her head game. His dick was bronzed and its purple helmet looked filled with desire. His leg shook and Bambi smiled.

She was pulling out all her tricks. Taking the ice out of Vincent's drink, Bambi place the cube into her mouth. Then she took Vincent's balls into her mouth with the ice and began sucking on them. After Bambi was satisfied she ran her cold tongue up Vincent's dick until she reached the tip. Bambi crushed the ice on her mouth before taking Vincent's throbbing dick into her mouth.

While Bambi's head was quickly bobbing up and down, her hands were all over Vincent's ass. In one quick motion Bambi spread Vincent's cheeks and stuck her index finger in his rectum causing Vincent to moan loudly ejaculating in her mouth. The crowd went berserk with disbelief over Bambi's bold move. Vincent's unmanly reaction brought the house down in laughter. Thirty seconds later, Big Heavy let his load bust all over Porsha's face and tits. It drew a loud applause from the crowd but Porsha was pissed. She cursed him out and stormed off the stage. Big Heavy got himself together before going to apologize to Porsha and giving her an extra two hundred dollars.

Five minutes later, an exhausted Barbie made the young man explode. Her jaw was so sore that there were tears in her eyes. The crowd talked about the contest for weeks. It was another feather in Tameka's hat.

CHAPTER TWELVE

Spring '01 was in full swing. While the beginning of April was showering the women with plenty of money, the end of April was turning out to be a different story. It took three weeks for the buzz about the dick-sucking contest to fade out. During those three weeks the club stayed filled beyond its capacity with new customers. Tameka was proud of herself for bringing the new clientele into the club but with not only the buzz about the club now gone, but also the new clientele, Tameka was desperately looking for another way to put the club back on the tongues of all.

There were always challenges. Tameka was going around the club greeting customers, when she overheard a customer saying,

"Yeah Chuck, the only thing this little club missing is Desire."

Tameka smiled and placed her hand on the customer's shoulder.

"Excuse me for being rude but who is Desire?"

The man glanced up at Tameka and smiled back.

"She's a stripper like y'all. But unlike y'all, Desire is singlehandedly putting The Lady Fox on the map."

"She's turning tricks like that?" Tameka asked.

"Nah, she don't even get down like that. People go just to watch her dance," Chuck laughed.

"Dance…?" Tameka asked obviously upset. "We up in here butt naked, selling our souls trying to make it. And y'all going to spend money that y'all could be giving to us, in a regular strip club with a stripper who only dances? Shit, we need to change up our format. What kind of dancing she do?"

"Belly-dancing," the man said quietly. "She moves her body like no other woman I've ever seen."

Tameka stared at the man in disbelief. Chuck noticed Tameka's expression and spoke up.

"You see it's more than just belly dancing with Desire. It's everything about her. She intoxicates you with her walk, her talk, her look." Chuck paused before adding. "And the snake makes her that much more unapproachable."

"Snake…?" Tameka asked in shock. "The bitch dances with a snake…?" Both men nodded their heads. "I don't even want to hear anymore," she said, walking in Anna Marie's direction.

Before Tameka reached Anna Marie she stopped and turned back around. Tameka decided it would be better if everyone got a good night's sleep before she informed them about their latest obstacle.

The next day came, and she couldn't wait to tell the other women what she had heard about Desire. Tameka was hoping her coworkers would keep an open mind, and hear what she had to say. She was wrong.

"The money ain't flowing like it used to, Tameka," Renee said, looking at the other women. "We barely making fifteen hundred a night and now you want to bring in another dancer? That's crazy."

A frown formed, staining Tameka's face.

"I took you from making what-one, two hundred a night to one to three G's a night. And I'm crazy? I'm crazy all right, crazy for hiring yo sorry ass."

"I don't know who the fuck you think you talking to, but I ain't one of these other muthafuckas that's scared of yo ass. So you needs to check that mouth o' yours," Renee said, jumping up from her chair.

"Or what…?" Tameka asked, standing up.

"C'mon Tameka, it ain't like that," Porsha said, getting between the two women.

"You right. The little tramp ain't even worth it," Tameka said, nodding.

"Whatever bitch," Renee said, rolling her eyes.

"Enough, enough, enough," Anna Marie said, standing. "I'm not gon' be up in here dancing on no empty stomach. Quit trippin' and let's just put this to a vote and be done with it."

"A vote not gon' bring our customers back, Desire will," Tameka said, looking around the room. "I know y'all want to go eat before it gets too late. I'm not trying to hold that up. All I'm asking is that we at least check out the competition, and if she's what they say she is we put her on the team. We grown folks here…"

"That sounds fair," Porsha said, pulling out her cars keys. "Now let's go eat, please."

All the women got up to leave. Tameka blew a kiss at Renee and whispered, "Bitch…"

Renee rolled her eyes and continued out the club with the rest of the women. Tameka already saw Desire as part of the team. If Desire was putting a no-name club on the map, Tameka couldn't wait to see what she would do for Ass By The Pound.

Unfortunately, Tameka had to wait until Victoria took her final exams before she, Victoria, and Anna Marie would actually go see Desire. Victoria aced her first semester in college by avoiding all the trivial things, until after she took all of her exams.

This semester would be no different. Victoria wasn't about to let Tameka, Desire or any other person pull her away from her studies. She was also forced to put her relationship with Kenneth on hold. Kenneth understood, but Victoria still yearned for their secret meetings. If it wasn't for the difficulties she was having preparing for her Geology 101 class, she would have squeezed an hour in her schedule for Kenneth. Her Geology class was affecting her so much, Victoria started stressing and this brought back her nightmares.

Victoria fell asleep with her Geology notes in hand. She had only been sleeping for an hour before the dreams kicked in. Victoria was once again a little six or seven year old girl, taking a rainbow lollipop from the grown man.

"Thank you," a young Victoria said.

The man's hand was outside of the young Victoria's panties. The young Victoria and the grown Victoria both squirmed when the man pulled the young Victoria's panties to the side.

"Everything's going to be all right," he said, prying one of his fingers inside of her small opening.

"It hurts," the young Victoria said, crying.

The man took his finger out of Victoria and placed it to his lips.

"Shush, it's going to be all right," he said, pulling down his pants. "I have another lollipop for you, sweetie."

Victoria woke from her sleep in a puddle of sweat.

"What's wrong with me?" she asked, getting out of her bed.

Victoria grabbed a nightgown and headed to the bathroom. She took a long, hot bath. Victoria spent the rest of the night studying for her exams. She was going to take the weekend off, but desperately wanted to see Kenneth. He was the only person who could put Victoria's mind at ease concerning her final exams.

She had completed her routine and walked around the club, headed to Kenneth's table when Vincent stopped her.

"What's up with a lap dance?" Vincent asked.

Victoria smiled and said, "Thank you, but no thank you. I'm on something else right now."

Vincent looked at the two men sitting at his table and said, "I know this bitch just didn't play me. Did she?"

"Damn right, she did," one of the men said, laughing.

"Bitch, do you know who the fuck I am?" Vincent asked, standing up. "I'm the man up in here."

Victoria was trying her hardest not to lose her composure. She reached for an apology and said, "Fo' real, if I offended you, I apologize. But I've got another customer ahead of you. I'll get to you later, okay?"

"Nah bitch, you'll get to me now," Vincent said, shaking his head.

"Is there a problem?" Kenneth asked, walking up.

Victoria didn't want to cause a scene especially with Tameka floating around.

"Um, there's no problem. Everything is fine."

"This don't concern you. Why don't you do what you do best and quit while you're ahead," Vincent said with a frown on his mug.

The two men sitting at Vincent's table laughed, but Kenneth didn't find the comment humorous. "Don't hate on me because I was smart enough to get mines and get out. But ain't you in the wrong club?" Kenneth asked.

"What you mean by that?" Vincent asked, looking confused.

"I mean, you got women sticking things in yo ass, making you scream like a bitch. I just thought you might feel more comfortable in a gay club," Kenneth said, looking directly in Vincent's eyes.

Victoria laughed while Vincent charged Kenneth.

"You muthafucka... I'm a kill you!" He shouted.

Kenneth grabbed Victoria and put her behind him. Vincent threw a hook and missed wildly. Kenneth ducked, and threw a hook of his own. The punch landed on Vincent's solar plexus, causing him to double over. Kenneth then connected to Vincent's face with a one-two that sent Vincent to the floor. The two men sitting at Vincent's table jumped up, but before they could charge Kenneth, J.T. rushed to Kenneth's side causing the two men to pause.

"Ain't you gon' do sump'n?" Tameka asked Pete.

"Hell nah. I ain't trying to get in the middle of that," Pete said shaking his head.

"What you mean?" Tameka asked.

"Girl, are you serious? J.T. is the biggest dealer in the city, and Kenneth probably still got more money and connections than him. Vincent is just crazy," Pete said, staring at Tameka.

"I don't give a damn about who got what. Kenneth's ass gots to go!" Tameka said, storming off.

Vincent was on the floor unconscious and slob was running out of his mouth. J.T. looked down at Vincent, and then at the two men.

"Get yo man, and get the fuck up outta here."

When the two men collected Vincent, Tameka said, "That sounds like a good idea to me. Kenneth, you just cost us about four, five thousand dollars so you gots to go too."

"Don't hate me for being a real man," Kenneth said, reaching into his pocket and pulling out a fat roll of hundred dollar bills. "This should cover it," he said, tossing the money to Tameka. Kenneth then turned to Victoria. "Make sure she share that with y'all."

He blew Tameka a kiss and left. Victoria didn't call him then but ended up telephoning him that night. Her concern wasn't over the fight but rather why he antagonized Tameka. Kenneth took Victoria's mind off Tameka and his beef. He put it back where it belonged, on her final exams. Victoria did focus, and spent the entire week taking her exams.

The weeks that followed really challenged the women. Summer was less than one month away and the patronage of Ass By The Pound's was in rapid decline. The Feds did a sweep of all the drug dealers they had under surveillance in the county, and arrested over half of Ass By The Pound's regular patrons. With money tight, the club was forced to lower their standard and accept any paying customers.

"This some bullshit," Barbie said, changing her clothes. "I'm tired of dancing for these broke-ass niggas."

"Girl quit complaining. You still make more money in three nights than six nights in any other club," Renee said before walking out to greet the customers.

When Renee left, Barbie turned to Porsha and said, "I got something for that bitch tonight. You just wait and see."

"What you got planned?" Porsha asked anxiously.

"I'm a slip that stuck-up ass bitch some X, and have her ass eat my pussy."

"I'm with that," Porsha said, smiling. "Let me know if you need my help, girl."

"I will," Barbie said, walking out of the dressing room.

The night was filled with the same crowd the club had grown accustomed to. The nights of bullshitting two and three hours and still make two and three thousand dollars were now gone. The women were forced to work extra hard if they expected to make anything over one thousand dollars. While the crowd had changed, so did Renee's routine.

Renee had never been the drinking type, but since she felt drained after her routine on stage Renee would go to O.J. and order a shot of Hennessy. On this particular night Barbie was waiting for her at the bar. When O.J. gave Renee her drink Barbie signaled for Porsha.

"What's up girl?" Porsha asked, walking up. "Tough crowd, huh...?"

Renee turned her back and started conversing with Porsha. She left her drink unattended. Barbie quickly broke the pill and dropped it into Renee's glass, swirling it with her index finger. She licked her finger. Porsha continued to talk to Renee until Pete started clearing the customers out. Barbie grabbed her glass of gin and made a toast with Renee.

"Truce..." Barbie said before downing her drink.

Barbie informed Tameka earlier in the evening that she would lock up at the end of the night. Now that the Ecstasy pill was in Renee's system, Barbie was hurrying everyone. Tameka, Porsha, Barbie and Renee were the only ones remaining after closing. The pill had Renee already feeling horny. Each time Renee touched herself sensations went through her whole body. Tameka looked at Renee and asked, "What's wrong with you?"

Instead of Renee answering, Barbie jumped into the conversation and said, "She's alright. You can go ahead and catch up with Victoria."

"Nah, sump'n going down... Is that bitch drunk?" Tameka asked, her curiosity piquing.

"She high on that X," Porsha blurted out.

"Oh, y'all tried to sneak in a little session without me," Tameka said, walking up to Barbie.

"Nah Tameka. It ain't even like that," Barbie said, backing away. "I didn't think you wanted to be down with some shit like this."

"You gots to be kidding me, we all grown, I wanna party too," Tameka said, walking over to Renee. She placed her hand on Renee's pussy.

"Hmm... Yes," Renee moaned.

"This gon' be too easy," Tameka smiled devilishly.

"Yeah," Barbie said, smiling. "Like taking candy from a baby..."

"Nobody touches her until I get back," Tameka ordered, grabbing her keys and leaving. A few minutes later, Tameka returned with her goody-bag and said, "Now let the party begin."

Barbie and Porsha waited to follow Tameka's lead. Tameka walked up to Renee and said, "I knew yo ass liked women."

Tameka gave Renee a long, passionate kiss before laying her down on the stage. Renee was already wet and Tameka went straight for Renee's pussy.

"Ooh wee, her shit smell sweet," Tameka whistled, before burying her face in Renee's pussy.

Tameka tongue lapped over Renee's clit again and again. Porsha could watch no longer so she got behind and started licking Tameka's asshole.

"Oh, ah..." Tameka moaned as Porsha's tongue entered her asshole.

She had to take a break from licking Renee's pussy to fully enjoy her lover's tongue. Porsha tossed Tameka's salad, one hand rubbing Tameka's clit. The move made Tameka moan louder before she focused back on Renee's pussy.

Feeling left out, Barbie went to Tameka's bag and got a six inch strap-on dildo. She tightened it around her pelvis. Barbie went straight to Porsha who was already on her knees and stuck all six inches inside of her exposed, dripping pussy.

"Um, that feels good!" Porsha said, meeting Barbie's thrust by pushing her butt back. Porsha and Barbie were in rhythm. Porsha focused back on Tameka's ass and pussy. Renee climaxed like no other woman Tameka had ever seen.

"Ooh... Ah oh God... Yes!" Renee sighed.

The sight of Renee's pussy gushing like a geyser excited Tameka so much, she climaxed.

"Damn baby, you ain't never came that hard," Porsha said, staying in rhythm with Barbie.

"You just felt so good to me baby," Tameka smiled, sucking Porsha's lips.

Tameka stared at Renee's body. She was still writhing with lust and tameka smiled and said, "Lemme see if this bitch can use that tongue of hers for something other than talking shit."

Tameka stood over Renee who was still lying on the stage and smiled. Without warning, Tameka squatted down bringing her pussy in contact with Renee's mouth. Renee pushed Tameka away and licked her lips.

"I don't like the taste of that."

Tameka was shocked. That was the first time someone had ever dissed Tameka's pussy. Tameka stormed over to her goodie bag and pulled out a ten inch strap on dildo.

"Let's see if you like this," she said, strapping the dildo in place.

Renee opened her legs, smiled and said, "Come to mama."

Tameka roughly turned Renee over and pulled her onto all fours. She spanked her ass before thrusting deep into her pussy.

"Take this bitch!" Tameka said, ramming Renee with all ten inches.

"Bitch, you done lost yo mind!" Renee said, trying to get away from the dildo.

Tameka grabbed Renee by the waist. Grunting, she said, "Uh, uh. You asked for this." Tameka rammed all ten inches inside of Renee again and again.

"I ain't with this shit," Barbie said, pulling her dildo out of Porsha. "This shit getting kinda criminal."

"It was criminal when you slipped her the Ecstasy. Just get the fuck outta here and watch the show, bitch!"

Porsha stared at the carnal act with a frown of dissatisfaction on her face. Barbie sat down with Porsha and watched Tameka cram the ten inch dildo inside of Renee over and over again. Renee gave up fighting and decided to let Tameka have her way with her.

Sweat began to drop from Tameka's body as she continued to go in and out of Renee. Tameka smacked Renee on the ass screaming, "I got something real special for you."

Tameka pulled the dildo out of Renee, and ran her fingers up the dildo collecting Renee's juices. Tameka took the juices and spread them on the outside of Renee's asshole. As soon as Tameka stuck one of her fingers inside of Renee's asshole, Renee jumped.

"Oh hell no," Renee said, collecting her clothes. "Bitch, you done lost yo damn mind. You not about to stick that plastic shit up in my asshole, you sex-crazy…!"

"I'll catch you another time," Tameka said, taking the dildo off. "I'm about to take a shower anyway."

Barbie and Porsha joined Tameka in the shower. Renee hurriedly got dressed and left.

CHAPTER THIRTEEN

One month passed and no one had either seen or heard from Renee. Not only did Renee quit her stripping job with the ladies but she also quit her job at the record store with Anna Marie. At first Anna Marie was concerned something bad had happened to Renee. Maybe she went back to her baby's father. Anna Marie searched the newspapers for two straight weeks half hoping to read something about Renee. After finding nothing in the papers and constantly hearing Tameka saying she was all right, Anna Marie decided to stop focusing on the whereabouts of Renee. She changed her focus to the pending summer about to blast off.

Bambi, Barbie, Porsha and Tameka were all excited that Renee was gone. The reason Bambi, Barbie and Porsha were glad Renee was out of the picture was because one less dancer meant a little more money for the three of them. Tameka on the other hand was glad for other reasons. She was tired of Renee's disrespect, superior attitude and sneakiness. Renee's departure meant Tameka could now recruit Desire to fill Renee's spot and that made Tameka the happiest.

When she brought the Desire issue up again, Tameka faced resistance from all the women. She knew Bambi, Barbie, Porsha and Tonya suffered a financial loss when the Feds arrested the club's big tippers. They were making more money in Renee's absence so they would be against the hiring of another dancer. Tameka couldn't understand why Victoria and Anna Marie were against the idea. The three of them never stopped making good money. Tameka stood firm on the hiring of Desire. In the end Victoria and Anna Marie agreed to at least go with Tameka to see Desire's routine.

It was a Thursday night when Tameka, Victoria and Anna Marie went to watch Desire's routine. The Lady Fox was filled with the customers from all over, even some of the Ass By The Pound's most faithful customers were in attendance. Tameka stood in shock as she watched Vincent get a lap dance from a gorgeous, honey-brown woman.

"See, that's why I wanted to add more days. Bitches up in here getting our money," Tameka said, turning to Anna Marie.

Anna Marie rolled her eyes at Tameka and said, "Quit trippin', girl. We ain't the only dancers in the world, so we can't get all the money."

Tameka motioned for a waitress and said, "I can't believe you don't care that some of our biggest customers are up in here giving away money that we should be getting tomorrow."

"No, I don't care," Anna Marie said nonchalantly.

"Fo' real, me neither, Tameka," Victoria said, looking around the club. "All of us are still making money. It's just slow money right now. But business will pick up."

Tameka waited until they ordered their drinks and the waitress left before responding.

"See, it's thinking like that that got us struggling." She paused and shook her head. "Yeah, we still making a little money, but Tonya, Porsha, Bambi and Barbie are struggling. We're all grown here, we falling off."

The waitress returned with their drinks and left. Tameka decided to wait until they saw Desire's routine before she pressed the issue any further. She sat back in her chair and enjoyed her drink while surveying the club. Tameka didn't see a woman fitting the description of Desire, but her eyes followed the pretty woman who was giving Vincent a lap dance earlier. She was now working the crowd. Tameka kept her eyes on the woman's movements, and was impressed how she worked the customers. Making a mental note, Tameka wanted to come back by herself and see if the woman was interested in becoming friends with benefits.

Two hours passed and the three women did not see one woman that even resembled Desire. While Victoria was only on her second drink, Anna Marie was on her sixth shot of Hennessy. Anna Marie was growing more impatient by the minute. It was starting to show.

"Quit trippin', girl… This here some bullshit," Anna Marie said, getting up. "This bitch got us waiting on her like she a star or sump'n. I ain't no muthfuckin groupie. I'm a be up outta here."

Before Tameka could stop Anna Marie, the DJ announced, "Now coming to the stage for all of y'all viewing pleasure. The beautiful, exotic… The woman of every man's dreams—

"Desire…"

"Quit trippin', girl…" Anna Marie said and the crowd went wild.

Desire came out, and instantly caught everyone's full attention. Stunningly beautiful, Desire stood five-foot six and weighed one hundred and thirty pounds. She had long black hair and light brown eyes. Her creamy vanilla complexion was flawless. Desire's lithe, curvy frame swayed like no other woman's body. She mesmerized the crowd with her beautiful, rhythmic hips. Unlike the other strippers, Desire's routine wasn't limited to just the stage. She waded through the club, softly landing at each table. Collecting tips, she continued mesmerizing the audience with her calming appeal and those hips.

Desire finally made it to Tameka's table. She was shocked when Tameka pulled out a hundred dollar bill, kissed it and handed it to her.

"We need to talk business," Tameka said, giving Desire a wink and a smile.

Desire nodded her head and continued to work the crowd. Disappearing in the back, Tameka thought she had finished her routine. She was wrong.

The sexy dancer reappeared with a five foot long white python wrapped around her arms and neck. Anna Marie jumped up from the table.

"Quit trippin', girl. Oh hell… That bitch better stay the fuck away from me. And she definitely ain't bringing that snake up in the club."

"We grown, girl. Sit yo ass down."

Embarrassed by Anna Marie, Tameka rolling her eyes watching her inebriated friend taking a seat. They sat quietly admiring the enchantment of the dancer with the snake. Later after her routine was complete, the dancer minus the snake spoke with Tameka.

"You wanted to talk with me?" Desire asked, displaying a distinct accent.

"I love your routine," Tameka smiled, greeting the dancer.

"Thank you," Desire said.

"But I love your accent even more. Where are you from?"

"India," Desire said proudly. "But we moved to the United Stated when I was three."

"Fo' real, how long have you been dancing?"

"As soon as I could walk… My mom used to say I went straight from crawling to dancing. It's so much an integral part of our culture." Desire's face lit up.

"Quit trippin', girl. That must be soo nice," Anna Marie said sarcastically. "So have you heard of Ass By The Pound?"

"Of course, who hasn't? That's the competition."

"Quit trippin', girl. Competition…" Anna Marie said, laughing. "So you think this is a game?"

"I don't follow," Desire said with a look of confusion on her pretty face.

"Ah, don't pay her no mind. We grown and she's drunk."

"Quit trippin', girl. I ain't that drunk to know she thinks this shit is a game."

"I think I should be leaving now," Desire said, getting up from the table.

"Please wait," Tameka said, touching Desire's toned arm. "You haven't even heard my business proposal."

"I'm listening," Desire said, sitting back down.

"We are Ass By The Pound," Tameka said, pointing at Victoria, Anna Marie and herself. "And we're here to offer you a job."

"Oh no, I can't," Desire humbly smiled.

"I'm sure we can work something out. I know you making some money here, but we can guarantee you more money in less time," Tameka said proudly.

"I doubt that," Desire said, shaking her head. "You see, I have a solid contract with the owner. In five months, I will be part-owner."

Tameka was speechless, but Anna Marie wasn't. She looked around the table and found Tameka's stunned face.

"Anymore bright ideas?" she asked her.

"Ugh, shut up, you lush," Tameka said, staring at the gorgeous, honey brown complexioned woman again. "I may be down but I'm not out."

"What do you mean by that?" Victoria asked.

"You see that girl right there," Tameka said, pointing.

Desire along with the others gazed at the dancer Tameka was pointing at.

"That's Angel. She's very popular around here. You should ask her, she might take you up on your offer," Desire said. She got up and walked away.

"I've been watching her movements all night. And customers love her. We grown, if we can't get the queen, I say we take her princess. Either way we'll be bringing new clientele to Ass By The Pound."

"Quit trippin', I don't care anymore," Anna Marie said, sounding exhausted. "I just wanna get outta here."

"Go ahead and call her over. Fo' real, let's get this over with."

Tameka motioned for Angel to come over. This was the first time Tameka seen Angel up close, and truly it was the face that was angelic.

"Can we talk to you for a minute?" Tameka asked, wearing a warm smile.

Angel bent over and whispered, "I don't get down like that."

"Ha! I like her already," Anna Marie laughed.

"What you mean by that?" Tameka asked, taking offense. "I'm here to offer you a job, a better job. And you jump to a conclusion like that."

"My bad," Angel said softly. "But you'd be surprised at the things people ask me to do."

"Fo' real, we understand. But it's not even that type of party," Victoria assured Angel. "This is strictly on the up and up," she added.

"So what kind of job y'all talking about?" Angel asked with curiosity.

Victoria waited on Tameka to go into her sales pitch. Seemingly uninterested look all over her face, Tameka sat sulking at the table silent. Anna Marie was too drunk to be civil. Victoria was forced to do the talking.

"We're here to offer you a job with us."

"And exactly who're y'all?" Angel asked, perplexed.

"We are Ass By The Pound," Victoria said proudly. "Tameka saw you working the crowd and thought you'd be a perfect addition to our little team."

"I don't know," Angel said, looking around the club. "I know y'all making a little money, but I got a good set up here."

"A good set up...?" Tameka laughed. "I don't mean to be rude, but we all grown. How much do you make a week?"

"At least two G's," Angel proudly answered.

"That's peanuts, Angel. You can make that in one night with us. I'll tell you what, come by and dance tomorrow night at Ass By The Pound. If you like it, we cool. If you don't, we still cool," Tameka said, sitting back.

"Ain't no harm in trying to do better for myself," Angel said, smiling. "It's all about opportunity. Plus, I can't stand that stuck-up bitch Desire. She's a..." Angel let her voice trail off.

"One other thing," Tameka said, looking around the club. "You should let the customers up in here know where you're going to be dancing tomorrow night," Tameka said, giving Angel the club's address.

"Good idea," Angel said, getting up from the table. "I'm a go do that right now."

Tameka turned to Victoria and said, "Let's get this drunk-ass, mixed breed home."

"Fo' real, I heard that," Anna Marie said, staggering out the club.

The next day brought a few sad faces. Bambi, Barbie and Porsha were not their normal playful selves. They couldn't believe Tameka hired Angel.

From their understanding Desire would have brought new customers, a lot of new customers. The three women didn't understand the logic in hiring a no-name like Angel.

Setting the club up for the night's show, Barbie and Porsha kept rolling their eyes at Angel. The new dancer ignored the two women and continued wiping the tables down. After the club was ready for business, they went to a nearby Chinese restaurant where they quietly pigged out. The routine was something new to Angel, but something she was definitely feeling.

In less than one hour after opening its doors Ass By The Pound was filled to its capacity. Barbie and Porsha were impressed with the large turnout. They quickly realized the new faces were Angel's faithful customers. As with all the new dancers, Angel received a lot of attention from the customers. Barbie and Porsha were no longer rolling their eyes at Angel. Instead, the two women were congratulating Angel on getting that money. Angel may not have been Desire, but she was a dancer who brought her own following.

The night was hugely successful. A lot of money was made. Even no-rhythm Tonya had a feast. At first Angel was shocked. She had no clue that she would have to get butt naked in front of the crowd. After seeing how much money the others were making, she had no problem with the complete strip act. That night, Angel was not only the one who made the most money, but also became the newest addition to Ass By The Pound.

Two weeks later, the club was still thriving. Tameka wanted the praise for restoring the club back to its money making days, but the women wouldn't give it to her. Instead, they gave Angel the glory. It was her customers who had come to the rescue. Either way the women were taking advantage of the newfound patronage. One night right before closing a customer stopped Bambi as she walked by.

"Excuse me, Bambi. Can I talk to you for a minute?"

"What can I do for you?" Bambi asked and stopped walking.

"Me and my man, here… Ah, we just tryin' a spend some time with you tonight," the man said with a sheepish grin.

"I don't do that," Bambi said, shaking her head. "Ask Barbie, she'll do it."

"But I'm asking you," the man said, pulling out a huge knot of money. "You can set the price."

Bambi looked at the money for a few seconds thinking. The club was back to making money but she was trying to get away from dancing and stripping.

"Two thousand a piece," she said.

They both gave her wide-eyed stares then broke out in raucous laughter.

"Let's get real. Two thousand a piece is way too much. I'll give up two G's for the both of us."

Bambi thought for a minute and said, "Two g's for two hours."

"Deal," the man said, handing Bambi a piece of paper. "That's the hotel and room number. And by the way…" The man said, getting to his feet. "My name is Keon and this my little brother David."

The two men walked off while Bambi went to get ready. Forty-five minutes later Bambi was fully dressed inside the hotel room. Keon and David were dressed in nothing but their silk boxers.

"Drop that dress and let's get it on," David eagerly said.

"Yeah, time is money," Keon said, setting down his champagne bottle.

Bambi let the sun dress she was wearing drop to her feet, exposing her nude body.

"That's what I'm talking about," David said, approaching Bambi.

David walked up to Bambi and started caressing her breasts. Keon walked behind her and started rubbing his limp dick up and down her butt cheeks.

"Ah yeah," Bambi moaned.

She pulled David's boxers down revealing a hard, thin, seven-inch. Bambi bent over and stuck it in her mouth.

"Uh huh…" David groaned from the pleasure of Bambi's hot mouth on his dick.

She was busy wiggling her fat ass in front of Keon. He wasted no time in strapping up and sticking his nine inch inside of Bambi's moistness.

"Ooh yeah," Bambi screamed, pausing from sucking David's dick to enjoy the feel of Keon's throbbing manhood.

Bambi wasn't lying when she told Keon she wasn't a freak anymore. Before that night Bambi who hadn't had sex in over eight months was feeling Keon's dick working deep inside her womb.

Keon was slowly moving in and out of Bambi. She was trying her best to concentrate on David's dick in her hand. Bambi playfully stroked his balls. Bambi then ran her tongue from David's balls back up to his dick. When she reached the tip of his dick, Bambi slowly put all seven inches of pipe in her mouth.

After three long, powerful pulls, David busted his nut all down Bambi's throat. David pulled away from Bambi's grip. Keon went from slowly fucking Bambi to quick, powerful stroking.

Bam! Bam! Bam!

David heard the sound of Bambi's protruding ass hitting Keon's thighs every time he pulled her against him. A minute of speed fucking went by and both were breathing hard. Finally Bambi and Keon exploded at the same time. There was a ten minute recess. Bambi had just recovered when a butt-naked, Keon, walked in front of her.

"I need a little assistance," he said, pointing at his limp dick.

Bambi grabbed his dick and began to suck his balls while jacking him off. In a matter of seconds Keon was at full attention and rearing to go.

"So what's next?" Bambi asked.

"I want that brown eye while David hittin' the pussy," Keon smiled.

"Uh, uh, you too big... David maybe, but not you," Bambi said, shaking her head.

"Alright, how we gon' do this?" David asked.

"Standing," Bambi said, getting up.

She grabbed the KY Jelly from her bag on the nightstand, and greased her asshole. Then she greased David's dick and slowly guided him into her asshole. Bambi then raised her left leg and placed it on Keon's shoulder, allowing him easy access to her pussy. David used his hands to spread

Bambi's ass cheeks apart and was hitting it. Once the two men found a rhythm, the train was gone and they all enjoyed the ride. The evening ended with the tongue action of Bambi. She sucked both Keon and David's dick. David got so horny he bent her over and fucked her pussy hard. Bambi left the hotel refreshed and wanting more.

CHAPTER FOURTEEN

The summer may have started off badly for Ass By The Pound, but it definitely didn't end on that note. Adding Angel to the club's roster caused business to improve and stayed on the increase. Angel adjusted well to the club's rules and became one of the favorites among the customers. Of course Angel being a crowd favorite didn't sit well with Porsha and Barbie. Their hating on her went into effect.

The two women couldn't stand the fact that every night, since she had been there, Angel made more money than they did. In an attempt at making more money, Barbie and Porsha switched up their routines. They would sometimes dance together and brought the house down when they ate each other pussies on stage.

Freaky was an understatement when it came to what they were doing. Angel wasn't the type to bow out gracefully and kept changing her routine. She always kept the crowd anticipating her next routine. The competition between the three women not only helped them make more money, but also helped the entire bottom line of the club.

Not only did Victoria ace her final exams, but she and Tonya both made the Dean's list. The two went out and celebrated by themselves. Kenneth also found time to take Victoria out to do a little celebrating. The more Victoria and Kenneth saw of each other the closer the two became but no matter how close the two became, Victoria was still unable to express her true feelings. Kenneth was being patient and Victoria was hoping that he remained that way until she could figure out what was holding her back.

Summer was now over and colder weather was quickly approaching. It was time for the ladies to pack away their short shorts and pull out the winter clothes. Since Anna Marie was never the one to wear last year's fashion she convinced Tameka and Victoria to go clothes shopping with her at the mall. The three women were walking around the mall laughing and joking when they heard someone shouting.

"Look at them nasty bitches, stripping and stuff. And those two right there, they fucking dykes."

When Tameka, Victoria and Anna Marie turned around they saw their high school nemesis, Monique, standing with Cheryl and Tiffany.

"Stuck-up-ass-bitch! Who the fuck you talking to?" Tameka testily asked.

In high school Monique was considered to be a prissy type, and would have never talked crazy to Tameka. Monique had two, hefty looking women standing at her side. She thought the odds were in her favor.

"I'm talking to your lesbian-ass," Monique said with as much attitude as she could muster.

"I know this bitch just didn't... You got yo shit on you?" Tameka said to Anna Marie.

Anna Marie stayed ready for action and said, "Quitt trippin', girl. You know I don't leave home without it," Anna Marie said, smiling.

"Let's bring it to these bitches," Tameka said, stepping to Monique. "Yo mouth just got yo ass in a lot of trouble, bitch!"

"Get out of my face! Who the fuck you think—" Monique said, pushing Tameka in the chest.

Tameka pulled out the straight razor and slashed Monique across the face. Monique couldn't say another word.

"Ah-ah-ah…!" Monique squealed wikd and loud as if she was a stuck pig. "This bitch done cut me. Do something," she ordered her mall crew.

Not wanting to mess with an armed woman, Tiffany ran straight at Anna Marie. Cheryl charged Victoria. Anna Marie eased her razor out of her pants pocket and tucked it behind her back. Tiffany was running so fast, that when Anna Marie flashed the blade it was too late.

"My face…! My face…!" Tiffany screamed.

Tiffany's screams caused Cheryl to stop and turn in time for Victoria to throw a right cross. Cheryl went back a couple steps and Victoria grabbed her hand.

"You bitch!" Cheryl said, charging Victoria and wrestling her to the ground.

Once Victoria was on the ground Cheryl sat on her putting all two hundred and ten pounds in Victoria's midsection. Down but definitely not out, Victoria started swinging wildly at Cheryl's face.

"Get this big bitch off me!"

Anna Marie rushed over and kicked Cheryl in the back of her head causing her to slide off of Victoria.

"Fo' real, it took you long enough. That bitch was squashing me like a grape."

The two laughed and turned around to see Tameka on top of Monique pounding away.

"Take that bitch. Who the lesbian now, huh bitch? You my bitch!"

Tameka managed to throw two more punches to Monique's face before she was tackled by mall security. All six women were detained until the local authorities arrived. The six women were taken to the police station where they were questioned. Tameka, Victoria and Anna Marie stuck to the street code by saying nothing while Monique, Cheryl and Tiffany spilled their guts. The three women reported that they were assaulted by Tameka, Victoria and Anna Marie for no reason and they wished to press charges. Monique, Cheryl and Tiffany were released while Tameka, Victoria and Anna Marie were transported to the county jail.

The county jail was an experience like no other. Tameka, Victoria and Anna Marie were stuck in a holding tank with five other women. Three of the women had prostitution charges while the other two women had theft charges. One of the prostitutes looked like a normal girl while the other two looked liked crack-heads. One of the crack-head looking prostitutes kept scratching her pubic area. It wasn't until the women were processed that everyone found out she had a dose of crabs.

The women were stripped of their clothes, and sprayed with a cold chemical. They stood freezing and Tameka was thinking she was seeing things.

"Oh hell nah," Tameka shouted, backing away. "This bitch got bugs dropping off her."

All of the other women backed away. They talked about the crack-head prostitute who looked at them with a smirk on her face.

"Don't act like y'all ain't never had crabs. Shit, I'd rather have crabs than some other shit."

"Quit trippin', bitch and shut yo nasty ass up!" Anna Marie said in disgust. "I know you selling pussy, but that shit right there don't make no sense. You suppose to have more pride in yourself than that."

The women continued trash talking until they were allowed to shower and dress. They were issued sheets, blankets and towels. Then they were escorted to their sections. Anna Marie and the crack-head prostitute were placed in a section together while Tameka was placed on the same floor, but in another section with the other two prostitutes. Victoria and the other two women were taken to another floor where they were put in the same section. This would be the ladies living arrangements until they went to court.

Tameka, Victoria and Anna Marie were forced to spend two days in the county before they went to court, and received a bond. Tameka's charges were assault, assault with a deadly weapon and resisting arrest. Her bail was set at thirty-five thousand dollars, meaning she only needed ten percent to get out. Anna Marie had the same charges and bond as Tameka. Victoria was hit with only an assault charge, and her bail was set at twenty-five thousand dollars with only two thousand and five hundred dollars needed to be paid. Tameka told Victoria that she would have Pete pay both their bonds and to sit tight.

Tameka had a hard time tracking Pete down. It took her two hours to locate and tell him about their bonds. Pete didn't want to pay Victoria's bond, but it wasn't his money and he reluctantly agreed. Anna Marie didn't have any problems locating J.T. She told him about their bonds and he was on his way.

Anna Marie and Victoria ended up in the dressing area together. They knew Tameka would be coming down any minute, but she never showed. The two women were released only to find J.T. and Kenneth waiting. Victoria rushed into Kenneth's arms.

"What are you doing here?" she asked softly.

"Picking up my jailbird," Kenneth smiled.

"Fo' real, I ain't no jailbird, I'm a political prisoner. But we need to get out of here before Pete shows up," Victoria said.

"Quit trippin', girl. But I'm with you on that one," Anna Marie said, grabbing J.T.'s hand. "I ain't trying to fuck nobody else up. Plus, I ain't got my blade on me."

The four of them left just in time for Pete to see them from his car. He knew Victoria was seeing Kenneth, but he convinced himself that it wasn't his place to tell Tameka. Pete waited until the four left. Then he went to pay Tameka's bond. When Tameka finally got released, she was confused.

"Where's Victoria?" she asked.

"Gone," Pete said nonchalantly.

"What you mean, gone?" Tameka asked, perplexed.

"I mean she's not here," Pete said, walking away. "I guess Anna Marie paid her bond. She's gone too."

"Bitches couldn't even wait on me," Tameka said, walking out the county doors.

October 2001 meant it was time for the Circus City Classic. This was one of the biggest Black college football events. People from all over would travel to Indianapolis, Indiana where the game was always held. Kenneth, J.T., Victoria and Anna Marie were there enjoying the game. It was an every year event for Kenneth and J.T. They brought Victoria and Anna Marie along to spend some quality time together away from the madness of the city and Tameka.

The game was played Saturday night in the RCA Dome. Instead of watching the game and returning to Gary, the four individuals decided to spend the night in Indianapolis. Sunday night they would go back home in time for Victoria and Anna Marie to make some money at the club. Kenneth and J.T. didn't like the girls stripping, they respected the fact that Victoria and Anna Marie weren't living off them. Instead they were independent women.

The game was off the chain, but the halftime show was the highlight of the night. Marching bands from both schools performed at the highest level possible. After the game the four went out to eat before ending up at their hotel. Kenneth and Victoria had a suite with a Jacuzzi. J.T. and Anna Marie settled for a room with a regular hot tub.

Kenneth and Victoria were lying in their bed when Kenneth rolled over and began kissing Victoria. She offered no resistance, but when Kenneth went for her jeans, Victoria pulled away.

"Fo' real, I'm sorry, Kenneth. I can't," Victoria said, looking down at the bed. "I don't know what's wrong with me."

"Hey, it's okay. I can wait until you're ready," Kenneth said, gently rubbing her face.

"Thank you for being such a patient man," Victoria said with her head on Kenneth's chest. The two spent the night talking until they fell asleep in each other's arms.

J.T. and Anna Marie had never had sex with each other, but there was no nervousness between the two. J.T. decided to flip the script by giving Anna Marie a strip tease show followed by a lap dance. Anna Marie was so turned on at J.T.'s efforts that she quickly got undressed and tackled J.T. on the bed.

"Damn ma, you just gon' take the dick?" J.T. asked playfully.

Anna Marie took a break from kissing J.T. all over his face and said, "Quit trippin', boy. Right now I'm a horny little devil and only you can satisfy me."

Anna Marie kissed his chest, moving down to his stomach and finally arriving at his fully erect eight inch dick. She wrapped her lips around J.T.'s dick, taking him deep into her mouth.

"Oh sh…" J.T. moaned from the hotness of Anna Marie's mouth.

It took all the strength he had to pull Anna Marie away from his dick. She looked at him wearing nothing but a confused expression.

"What's wrong?" she asked.

"Nothing sweetheart," J.T. said, trying to catch his breath. "It's just that I want to please you too. Let's sixty-nine," he smiled.

Anna Marie quickly got on top of J.T. and went to work, licking his dick up. She finally put J.T.'s dick all the way in her throat. J.T. was pleasuring Anna Marie by rubbing her clit with his thumb. He stuck his tongue deep into her moistened pussy, twirling it around inside of her.

"Oh J.T. yes baby that's it, that's it," Anna Marie moaned.

J.T. slowly licked Anna Marie's clit. The strokes of his tongue were not only slow, but they were also powerful.

"Oh yes, God Oh, oh… Yes!" Anna Marie moaned loudly.

J.T. took her clit in his mouth and started sucking it and she lost her composure, erupting in an explosive orgasm in J.T.'s face. She farted loudly at the end.

Anna Marie covered her face with her hands in obvious embarrassment. She had never come so hard in her life and the force made her fart.

"This is soo embarrassing…" she started.

"It's cool baby," J.T. said, smiling. "I'm glad you showed me how much you appreciated my efforts."

Anna Marie smiled and J.T. went back to sucking her clit. She sucked on J.T.'s balls while jerking his dick. Anna Marie placed his nuts in her mouth and hummed, sending electric-like sensation through J.T.'s body. She repeated the process and could feel J.T.'s dick beginning to swell. Anna

Marie quickly released J.T.'s nuts and placed his dick back in her mouth and began sucking. Her head bobbed up and down, taking all eight-inches inside her mouth. J.T. shot his load down Anna Marie's throat. She swallowed fast, licking her lips and not letting one drop get away.

The two sprawled across the bed catching their breath. It wasn't until Anna Marie rolled on top of J.T. that the silence was broken.

"That was only round one," Anna Marie said, grabbing J.T's semi-hard dick and eased it inside of her.

Her hips moved in a slow gyration. J.T. caressed her breast and she could feel J.T. swelling inside her moistness. Once fully erect, Anna Marie began to ride the dick like a mechanical bull. Anna Marie bent down softly kissing J.T. on his lips before placing her hands on his chest and speeding up the pace.

Her body sweated while moving up and down, each time going faster and faster. J.T. managed to get his thumb on Anna Marie's clit and kept it there. Anna Marie rode J.T. and he massaged her clit. In no time the two climaxed in unison. Anna Marie looked over at J.T. and smiled.

"I love you, J.T."

She heard the words slipping out of her mouth befoe she could stop them. It was something she never thought she could ever mean.

"I love you too."

Lying in his arms, Anna Marie continued to make sweet love for the rest of the night, through the early morn.

CHAPTER FIFTEEN

Quickly days turned into weeks, after they were released from the county jail. During their time at the County jail, life opened up their eyes to more important things. With the possibility of doing jail time over their heads, Tameka, Victoria and Anna Marie started focusing on enjoying their freedom. Tameka stopped worrying about the club, focusing on her and Victoria's relationship. She knew how to be a romantic when she needed to be, but Victoria wasn't falling for Tameka's tactics. Tameka never got discouraged. She just tried harder.

The New Year was only three days away and there had been no snow so far in Gary, Indiana. Victoria was bummed out because she loved the snow. To her, Christmas wasn't Christmas without snow. In hopes of cheering up Victoria, Kenneth took Victoria to her favorite restaurant.

Delicious was located in Lake Station, Indiana, next to a bunch of no name strip clubs. Despite the poor location of the restaurant, the food at Delicious was some of the best Victoria ever tasted. She and Kenneth were enjoying the food, and it suddenly began to snow.

"Fo' real, look," Victoria excitedly said, pointing. "It's snowing."

Kenneth looked out the window and saw the big, white flurries coming down.

"So it is. I guess you real happy now, huh?"

"Not yet," Victoria said, getting up from the table. "Come outside with me."

"What ...?"

Kenneth paid their bill and joined Victoria outside in the fresh snow.

"Isn't it beautiful?"

"Yes but the beauty is no match for yours," Kenneth said, his arms around Victoria's tiny waist. He lifted her up, swinging her body in the air.

"Stop," Victoria said, gigling like a school girl.

Kenneth was busy spinning her around. She giggled and tried to relax. Kenneth and Victoria were enjoying themselves and trouble drove by.

"I can't believe this nigga slipping like this," a man said, pulling into parking lot at Delicious.

"The snow gets more love than I do...?" Kenneth asked, putting Victoria down.

"Nah, you know it ain't like that. You know how I feel about you," Victoria said, smacking her lips.

"Why don't you tell me...?" Kenneth asked seriously.

Before Victoria had a chance to respond, she heard someone said, "Ain't life a bitch. Get yo muthafuckin hands up!"

Kenneth looked up and between clenched teeth said, "Vincent."

"That's right nigga!" Vincent said, waving a chrome .357 at Kenneth. "Now get yo hands up because it's payback time."

"Fo' real, I know this ain't about the club," Victoria said, easing behind Kenneth. "A little beat down ain't never hurt nobody."

Kenneth and Vincent both looked at Victoria.

"Let me handle this," Kenneth said, speaking softly to Victoria.

"Ain't shit to handle," Vincent said, stepping to Kenneth. "You a dead fuckin' man," Vincent smiled, raising his gun to take aim.

"Wait a minute, Vincent," Kenneth said, putting hands out in front of him. "You know if you kill me J.T. gon' kill you."

"Fuck J.T.!" Vincent shouted. "That nigga ain't shit. Plus, how he gon' know I'm the one who killed you? This bitch's dead too."

"Fo' real, if you kill me, you gotta kill all those witnesses looking at you in the restaurant window."

Vincent turned to look. Kenneth quickly seized the opportunity, grabbing Victoria and jumping behind a parked car. The two quickly began crawling away from Vincent. He turned back around to find no one standing in front of him.

"Where are you, Kenneth? You might as well get this over with. You can't hide."

Kenneth got Victoria to a place where he thought she would be safe. He pulled a 9mm from his back and said, "You stay here and don't come out unless I call you. You got that?"

"Yes," Victoria said, hugging Kenneth tightly. "Be careful."

"I will," Kenneth said, kissing Victoria on the forehead. Then he smiled and said, "I love you."

"I love you too," Victoria said with tears in her eyes.

Vincent was moving from car to car, trying to find Kenneth and Victoria. He knew if he let Kenneth get away, Kenneth would put a hit out on him immediately. Vincent continued to move from car to car. Each time Vincent came up empty, he became a little more desperate.

"Come on Kenneth, I was just playing," Vincent said, looking. "Why don't you come on out so we can talk?"

"Drop your gun, Vincent," Kenneth said, standing behind Vincent.

"I ain't dropping shit," Vincent said, turning quickly with his gun in his hand.

Kenneth waited until Vincent was completely turned around. He fired two bullets into Vincent's chest. Gasping for air, Vincent fell hard to the ground. Kenneth walked over to Vincent and said, "You heard what Scarface said, 'always look a man in the eyes before you kill him.'"

Kenneth then shot Vincent one more time in the chest before walking away. He ran over to Victoria, extending an arm.

"Come on, we gotta get out of here," he hurriedly said.

Victoria grabbed Kenneth's hand. The two ran to Kenneth's truck and left. After they were safely away from Delicious, Victoria turned to Kenneth.

"Fo' real, what happened?"

"What do you mean?" Kenneth asked. His eyes were fixed on the road.

"Did you kill Vincent?" Victoria asked flatly.

Kenneth looked over at Victoria and said, "Yes, I had to kill Vincent. And I'll do it again if it means protecting the woman I love."

Victoria sat in silence for a minute. She said, "Well, it was either him or us."

"Exactly," Kenneth said, smiling. "Now you know this has to be our little secret."

"I'll take it to my grave," Victoria said, looking deep into Kenneth's eyes. The rest of the night, the two rode in silence.

News of Vincent's demise became the talk of the town for the next couple of days. While the glory was being given to J.T.'s crew, J.T. knew better. He knew that Kenneth was responsible for Vincent's death. Kenneth was at Delicious the night Vincent died. J.T. spoke to Kenneth about Vincent's death.

"I won't mention it again," J.T. said. "My only concern is whether you will be able to trust Victoria."

"Victoria will keep the secret," Kenneth assured J.T.

New Year's Eve Ass By The Pound was the place to be. This was the club's second annual New Year's Eve party. There was a better turn out than last year. Some of the heavyweights arrested, were released on bond. They were in attendance. The house was filled to the max. This made it easy for Victoria and Kenneth to sneak out. They chilled outside in Kenneth's Denali, talking.

Meanwhile inside the club, Tameka was busy getting drunk with her brother, Pete.

"I'm telling you Pete, these bitches don't appreciate shit I've done for them," Tameka said, pouring herself another shot of Hennessy. "I took 'em bitches from getting pennies for dancing to getting twenties and fifties. But do I get any thanks? Hell nah."

"You really feeling yourself tonight, huh? Something must be bothering you. What's wrong?" Pete laughed.

"I'm horny. That's what's wrong," Tameka said, slamming her drink on the table. "I'm horny, and Victoria won't give me none."

Pete stopped laughing at his sister's drunkenness. He wanted badly to tell his sister about Victoria and Kenneth, but knew it was better for all of them if he remained silent on the issue.

"Fuck Victoria," Pete said, eyeing Anna Marie walking by.

"That's what I'm trying to do," Tameka chuckled.

"Nah, that's not what I meant," Pete said, shaking his head. He leaned against the table. "You got all this other pussy in here, and you focusing on one bitch. What's up with that?"

Tameka gulped down another shot of Hennessy. She started pouring herself another one. "Pete, Pete, Pete, I've had damn near every bitch in here. Me and you ran a train on Bambi. I fucked Barbie, and her pussy's stink. Porsha is my lover. And I can get the na-na from her anytime. I ain't got around to Tonya and Angel yet, but..."

"Anna Marie," a familiar voice called out.

Anna Marie had been secretly eavesdropping on Tameka and Pete's conversation ever since she heard Pete say "Fuck Victoria."

Then on hearing her name, Anna Marie jumped. When she turned around she was even more surprised.

"Renee," Anna Marie said, giving Renee a hug and continued. "Quit trippin', girl. Where the hell you been?"

Renee looked around the club and said, "Let's talk in the back."

Once they got in the back Anna Marie said, "Quit trippin', girl. I thought you was dead. What happened? Why did you just up and leave us hanging like that?"

Renee sat down on a bench and said, "I was date raped or something like that."

"Quit trippin', girl!" Anna Marie said in shock. "How…? Who? And what you mean something like that?"

Renee looked down at the floor the whole time she spoke.

"My last night here I got into it with Barbie. That bitch slipped me something. I guess she planned on her and Porsha having their way with me, but Tameka showed up and took control. Once she saw I was high the bitch ate me out, and then put her nasty pussy in my face." Renee paused and took a deep breath. "When I pushed that bitch off of me she got mad and pulled out her big ass dildo. She started fucking me with it. The bitch even tried to stick it in my ass, that's when I really started fighting and got away."

"Quit trippin', girl. What you doing now?" Anna Marie asked.

"Nothing, I just wanted Victoria to know all about Miss Bitch," Renee said, shrugging her shoulders.

"Quit trippin', girl. I got everything I need and more," Anna Marie said with a devilish smile. "What about you? What are you doing to eat?"

"I'm good. I strip on the internet now," Renee smiled.

"The internet…?" Anna Marie said repeated. "Quit trippin', girl, you getting paid off the internet?"

"Yeah girl, it's good legitimate money. You should try it. This ain't the only way, sister," Renee said, nodding her head.

"I already got one foot out the door," Anna Marie said and stood to her feet. "I'm about to find Victoria, but you ain't got to be a stranger. Call me sometime."

"I will," Renee said, giving Anna Marie a hug. "You take care."

"Quit trippin', girl. You do the same," Anna Marie said, returning Renee's hug.

Anna Marie spent about an hour searching for Victoria. It wasn't until after the club brought in 2002 that Anna Marie spotted Victoria. Victoria was in a corner talking to Tonya when Anna Marie walked up.

"Happy New Year… What's up?" Victoria asked.

"Happy New Year, girl, I need to talk to you alone," Anna Marie said, cutting her eyes at Tonya.

"It's cool. I'll catch up with y'all later," Tonya said taking the hint.

Once Tonya was out of earshot, Victoria asked impatiently. "Fo' real, what's up Anna Marie? Is something wrong?"

"Nah girl, everything's perfect. You're free," Anna Marie said and smiled.

"Would you just spit it out?" Victoria asked, growing impatient.

"Tameka's been cheating," Anna Marie said happily. "Cheating ain't even the word. That bitch done fucked Barbie, Porsha, Bambi and even raped Renee."

"Raped Renee…?" Victoria asked in surprise. "How do you know all this?"

"Tameka over there drinking and telling that to Pete, right now," Anna Marie said, pointing at Tameka. "I was listening to her brag about fucking Porsha when Renee snuck up behind me."

"Fo' real, Renee's here…?" Victoria interrupted.

"Quit trippin', girl. She was here," Anna Marie said, looking around the club. "She only stopped by to tell you that Tameka raped her, and wasn't good enough for you. So what you gon' do?"

"Fo' real, I didn't have any idea," Victoria said, glancing at Tameka and Pete yakking. "But whatever I decide, will be in my best interest."

"So you know the reason Renee quit?" Pete said after hearing Tameka tell him her version of what happened to Renee.

"Nah," Tameka said, shaking her head. "It wasn't my fault, or my plan. I just stumbled up on some pussy. We grown…"

Pete downed a shot of Hennessy then he said, "You my sister, and I'm with you no matter what, but how you just explained that shit to me it's called rape."

"Rape…?" Tameka said, laughing. "If I did something wrong then where is the police? Where the cops at…?"

Pete shook his head and said, "You need to get yo shit together. You slipping."

Tameka waved Pete off and got up from the table mumbling, "I'm slipping? Shit, how I'm slipping. I'm the one who keep us number one?"

The rest of the night Tameka expressed her true feelings to her coworkers. She fussed with Tonya, cursed at Angel and Bambi for no apparent reason. Then she went on to call Barbie every nasty name she could think of. Porsha was the only one able to calm Tameka. Victoria stayed far away watching everything.

CHAPTER SIXTEEN

Victoria thought long and hard about the things Anna Marie told her. The words, 'You're free', echoed in Victoria's mind, by the end of the New Year's Eve party, she had made her first new year's resolution. She would stop hiding her relationship with Kenneth from Tameka. Victoria's rage stirred her to flaunting the relationship, her mind knew better. She listened to her better judgment. Victoria decided to let Tameka provoke her one last time.

The month of January was being truly unkind to Anna Marie. She was having a hard time enjoying the New Year because she kept getting sick. Anna Marie could no longer enjoy the greasy food she liked to eat. Certain smells made her stomach queasy. She could no longer keep her liquor down.

Rumors spread amongst her coworkers, but Anna Marie paid them no mind. She couldn't be pregnant. It wasn't until Anna Marie realized she was three weeks late, that she called Victoria over, and took a home pregnancy test.

"Fo' real, tell me. What's the word?" Victoria asked anxiously.

Anna Marie shook her head and sighed. "I'm pregnant," she said, staring at the tube.

Victoria jumped off Anna Marie's bed screaming and shouting. She raced over to where Anna Marie stood frowning and said, "Fo' real, my girl's gonna be a mama."

Anna Marie tackled Victoria back onto the bed. "Quit trippin', girl. You know my mama downstairs."

"Fo' real, I'm sorry," Victoria said, hugging Anna Marie. "It's just that I'm soo happy for you, Anna Marie."

"Quit trippin', girl. Let me get up off of you. This here's some lesbian shit." Anna Marie stood with a frown on her face. "I don't even know if I'm going to keep it yet."

"What do you mean?" Victoria asked, sitting up in Anna Marie's bed.

"Quit trippin', girl. Me and J.T. never talked about having no kids. And I ain't raising no bad ass kid by myself."

Anna Marie plopped down on the bed next to Victoria. Smiling, Victoria put her arm around Anna Marie's shoulders.

"Fo' real, you know I ain't gone let you raise no child all by yourself. Auntie Victoria got yo back."

"Well Auntie Victoria better get used to babysitting," Anna Marie said, smiling. "Because after I have this child I'm still gonna have to get my party on."

"Fo' real, girl, you need Jesus," Victoria said, laughing.

"Quit trippin', girl," Anna Marie joined her laughing.

She wanted to know J.T.'s plans for the baby and wasted no time in telling him. He was ecstatic. This made Anna Marie very happy. Her delight soon faded when J.T, said, "I guess your strippin' days are finally over."

"And I guess your drug dealing days are finally over," Anna Marie shot back.

"Where did that come from?"

"Quit trippin', from the same place yo dumb ass question come from."

J.T. shook his head in disbelief.

"I don't believe this. This is not the first time I've asked you to quit strippin' but this is the first time you mentioned me quittin'."

"Stop, stop, stop," Anna Marie said, wrapping her arms around J.T.'s waist. "Before you start explaining yourself let me say this. My life doesn't revolve around strippin'."

"I wasn't…"

Anna Marie put her index finger to J.T.'s lips and said, "Let me finish." J.T. nodded his head and Anna Marie continued. "I strip because it's fun and because Victoria needs me to be there. It's not about the money. It never has been. There are some things more important to me than money and friendship is one." Anna Marie removed her finger from J.T.'s lip. "Quit trippin', I just need a little more time. I promise that I'll be through strippin' before I start showin'."

"You're promising that?" J.T. asked, smiling.

Anna Marie kissed J.T. on his lips and said, "I promise."

Anna Marie's pregnancy was not a secret. The customers entered the club and all congratulated Anna Marie on being pregnant. They all wished her the best. The customers' knowledge of her pregnancy puzzled Anna Marie. She had only told her family and two closest friends. Anna Marie paid the customers no mind. Spotting J.T. sitting in the back of the club watching her, she kept it moving.

"You're here early," Anna Marie said, bending over to kiss J.T. "I hope you not here stalking me."

"Nah, I ain't stalking you. I'm looking out for you and the baby. You know how wild it can get up in here," J.T. said, looking around the club.

"While you're playing bodyguard I'm a go make this money," Anna Marie said, sashaying away.

Two hours passed and Anna Marie had not made one dollar. Normally Anna Marie would have made almost one thousand dollars in two hours. Now that everyone knew she was pregnant, Anna Marie couldn't make anything. No one wanted a lap dance from a pregnant woman which doesn't make any sense either because Anna Marie was only seven weeks. She wasn't big and showing. It wasn't until Anna Marie noticed everyone toasting J.T. that she realized he had outsmarted her.

Anna Marie was sitting at a table by herself and Victoria walked up. She asked, "Fo' real, what's wrong? Are you having stomach pain or something?"

"Quit trippin', girl. I got a pain but it ain't in my stomach," Anna Marie said, staring at J.T. "Can you believe J.T. blackballed me?"

"Fo' real, blackballed you...?" Victoria asked.

"I really don't know. I guess he threatened the niggas up in here not to pay for a dance since I didn't quit like he wanted me to," Anna Marie said, shaking her head.

"Fo' real, he right," Victoria said, sitting down. "You shouldn't be working in here in your condition."

"Condition...?" Anna Marie said, laughing. "Quit trippin', girl. I'm not dying. And I'm not showing. One month not gon' kill me. Anyway, I got some unfinished business to handle."

"Fo' real, what's that?"

"Quit trippin', you it's you."

"Fo' real, me…? What unfinished business you got with me?"

Anna Marie looked Victoria directly in her confused eyes and said, "When I quit, I want you to quit. I don't want to leave you up in her with these scandalous bitches. You heard what they did to Renee."

Victoria grabbed Anna Marie's hand and said, "Fo' real, you've looked out for me long enough. Now let me look out for you. I'm not as weak as you think I am. I can handle Tameka and these other girls."

"Quit trippin', girl. I guess you've gotten a little tougher. Remember Tameka is still tougher. Why don't you call Renee and do the internet thing? We'll go in fifty-fifty."

Victoria spotted Kenneth and J.T. talking. She said, "I'll think about it. But for now, let's go see what's up with 'em fellas."

Tameka was no fool. She was guessing that Victoria and Anna Marie were up to something, but didn't know exactly what it was. Saying she was with Anna Marie, Victoria began coming home at two and three in the morning. Anna Marie would confirm Victoria's stories. Tameka suspected that the two would slip up. She started spying on them every chance she got. Tameka watched Victoria and Anna Marie heading to Kenneth and J.T.'s table. Victoria sat in Kenneth's lap and gave him long, passionate kiss. Tameka couldn't believe her eyes. Without realizing it, she ran over to where they were.

"What the fuck is going on over here?" Tameka asked angrily.

Victoria smiled and said, "I'm working."

Tameka's eyes bulged. She was breathing harder and became even angrier. By the time she spoke again she was shouting.

"And what part of putting yo muthafuckin tongue in this niggas mouth is work? Tell me we grown here. What the fuck is up?"

Victoria looked at Anna Marie then at Kenneth and said, "Fo' real, I'm busted. It looks like I'm not as sneaky as you."

Victoria was staring directly in Tameka's eyes. She watched the frown setting on Tameka's face.

"Huh? Sneaky as me…? What the hell is you talking about?"

"Fo' real, hmm lemme see. Where shall I begin, or rather, who shall I begin with? Barbie, Bambi, Porsha or maybe raping Renee…"

Tameka was stunned, but jumped into battle mode. Hands on her hips, she defended herself.

"Wha- wha- what are you talking about? I ain't raped nobody."

"Fo' real, you just fucked 'em?" Victoria said sarcastically.

Tameka extended her hand and said, "Let's talk in private."

Victoria snatched her hand away. She said, "Fo' real. Don't touch me. You repulse me!"

To the surprise of everyone looking on, Tameka grabbed Victoria by her hair. She yanked her out of Kenneth's lap.

"Bitch who the fuck the think you talking to? I'll beat yo muthfuckin ass right up in here."

Kenneth didn't know what to do but Anna Marie did. She jumped up from her seat, and hit Tameka in the eye.

"Quit trippin', bitch, and let her go!"

Tameka stumbled backward. Clutching her face, she said, "Oh, it's like that? You cross me for her…?"

"Quit trippin', girl. I ain't cross you. You crossed yourself when you cheated on my girl," Anna Marie said, helping Victoria to her feet.

"After everything we been through, it's come to this? You let a nigga come between us?" Tameka asked, shaking her head and looking at Victoria.

"Us…?" Victoria laughed. "There was and never will be any us. I'm not gay. We have always been only best of friends."

"We grown here, what about that night in the apartment?"

"What about it?" Victoria said angrily. "You got me drunk and ate my pussy. Damn, I guess you are a rapist."

"Bitch fuck you!" Tameka said and threw a right hand that connected with Victoria's jaw.

Victoria stumbled back into Anna Marie. She shook her head and put her fists up. Tameka could tell Victoria was dazed and charged her. Kenneth stuck his foot out causing Tameka to trip, sliding in a heap at Victoria's feet.

Anna Marie immediately nudged Victoria in the back and said, "Quit trippin', girl. Kick that bitch's ass."

Victoria was hesitant at first, but regained her senses. She landed a kick to Tameka's mid section as hard as she could. Tameka moaned like a wounded animal and Victoria swiftly kicked her again.

"Fo' real, take that," Victoria said, kicking Tameka again.

Tameka waited until Victoria drew her leg back before leaping forward and snatching Victoria's planted foot. Victoria fell to the floor hard. Tameka wasted no time in climbing on top of Victoria and smacking her.

"You lil' bitch! I'm a teach yo ass who's the real boss!" Tameka said, smacking Victoria again and again.

Anna Marie managed to get behind Tameka and grabbed Tameka's hair, pulling her off Victoria. Rushing to her feet, Victoria attacked Tameka. She was defenseless since Anna Marie was still holding her hair. Victoria was swinging wildly at Tameka. Trying her best to keep Victoria away, Tameka was kicking at her. Victoria got a good shot on Tameka, and Anna Marie cheered.

"That's what I'm talking about. Quit trippin', girl and hit this bitch again."

Pete stood back long enough. He thought Porsha was going to help Tameka since they were lovers but Porsha did nothing. Pete grabbed Victoria by her waist.

"That's enough, Victoria. You won," Pete said, holding her.

"Let me go. Lemme go," Victoria repeated, trying to wiggle free.

Kenneth jumped up from his seat and said, "Get yo hands off my woman." He blasted Pete in the nose with a left hand. Pete let Victoria go and Victoria ran back at Tameka. Tameka flung her head back and caught Anna Marie in the forehead. Anna Marie let go of Tameka and grabbed her head.

"Quit trippin', bitch. I'm a kick yo ass!"

Tameka was pissed but not that pissed to hit a pregnant woman. She said, "If you wasn't pregnant, I'd kick yo ass."

"Do it!" Anna Marie screamed in her face.

Tameka thought Anna Marie was talking to her but Anna Marie was actually talking to Victoria. She was telling Victoria to hit Tameka in the back of her head with the Hennessy bottle she was holding. Pete snatched the bottle from Victoria. Tameka swung twice missing the first time, but connecting the second time, hitting Anna Marie's mouth.

Tameka smiled and said, "You asked for it."

"And you asked for this!" J.T. said before knocking Tameka out with a blow to her temple.

Pete saw his sister fall to the ground and threw the Hennessy at J.T. The bottle hit J.T. in the middle of his back which caused him to wince. He turned around only to be tackled by Pete.

"You bitch ass nigga!" Pete said, choking J.T.

Kenneth kicked Pete in the back of his head causing Pete to fall forward. Before Kenneth could do anything else O.J. and Boo Rock grabbed him.

"Get the fuck off me!" Kenneth shouted, trying to get free.

O.J. and Boo Rock were struggling with trying to keep Kenneth under control. J.T. and Anna Marie were stomping away at Pete. J.T. looked over at Anna Marie and stopped kicking Pete.

"That's enough, baby. That's enough. You know you have to be careful," he said.

"Fuck this black ass nigga." Anna Marie said, kicking Pete one last time. "Don't you ever fuck with mines again."

J.T. laughed and turned around to see his man hemmed up. J.T. was about to run over to help Kenneth, but Victoria beat him to it. She busted a beer bottle over Boo Rock's head.

"Take that!" she said, grabbing another bottle.

With Boo Rock no longer holding him, Kenneth easily grabbed O.J. and threw him over a table. Kenneth then walked up to Victoria.

"Let's get you outta here."

The two women looked around and saw all eyes were on them. Other dancers and customers were watching them in awe. Tonight everyone got a little more than they paid for. Victoria and Anna Marie went in the back to grab their things. When the two returned they overheard Kenneth saying Pete had to go. Victoria glanced at Anna Marie for a beat.

"Fo' real, Kenneth, that's not really necessary. He was just looking out for his sister."

"Quit trippin', man, it ain't that serious," Anna Marie added.

"Not serious…?" Kenneth said, looking around the club. "Look at this. This is as serious as it gets."

Victoria hugged Kenneth around his waist and looked up at him. She said, "Fo' real, this nothing. We've had worse fights than this. Let it go, for me baby."

Kenneth looked at J.T. then at Victoria and said, "For you, I'm going to leave it alone. But," Kenneth said, pausing for a couple beats. "If any one of them tries to get some get back you know what it is."

"Fo' real, baby. Let's go get some of my things from the apartment."

Tameka was just regaining consciousness as Kenneth, Victoria, J.T. and Ann Marie were leaving. She sat dazed on the floor. Pete walked over and asked, "Are you all right?"

Tameka looked up and said, "I'm a get them bitches. You just wait and see. Them bitches is mine."

CHAPTER SEVENTEEN

For the first time in a very long while, Victoria felt truly happy. No longer a captive of Tameka, she no longer sneaked around with Kenneth, Victoria was now living with him. Her first night of freedom was spent in Kenneth's bed and in his arms. He tried to be a gentleman and offered to get Victoria a place of her own, but after experiencing the peace she felt in Kenneth's arms, Victoria kindly declined. One week had passed and things were still lovely.

With Victoria and Anna Marie no longer working at the club Tameka was even more driven to succeed. She wasn't going to let their betrayal stop her from making more money. Tameka thought about hiring two other dancers, but decided to wait. She was still holding on to the hope that her friends would return. In the meantime she and the other women could make all the money they wanted.

If Anna Marie was nothing else she was a shit starter. Against J.T. and Victoria's will Anna Marie went to pay Tameka a visit at the club. All eyes were on Anna Marie when she walked through Ass By The Pound and while the music didn't stop, the dancers most certainly did.

"Well, well, well. Look who decided to grace us with her presence," Tameka greeted Anna Marie. "It's Judas herself."

"I guess you'd call me whatever since you can't call Victoria," Anna Marie said and paused. "You know, she's looking better than ever now that she's away from you," Anna Marie said with a wicked smile.

"What the fuck do you want? Why are you here?" Tameka asked, frowning.

"I just wanted to tell you to you to your face. I quit. I quit stripping here and I'm done being your friend."

"I don't give a fuck! We're all grown. It's your loss," Tameka said, rubbing her fingers together.

Anna Marie was about to walk away, she said, "Oh yeah, the same goes for Victoria too. She doesn't want to see you ever again."

Tameka threw daggers, watching Anna Marie exiting the club. Once Anna Marie was gone, Porsha walked over to Tameka and said, "Fuck 'em! We don't need them to make this club work. You're the brains, anyway."

"You're right. We don't need 'em. Backstabbing bitches! Shit, look around, we still getting paid," Tameka said with a half smile clinging to her lips.

"That's right, baby. It's their loss. We still winning," Porsha said, kissing Tameka on the cheek.

Victoria used her time away from Tameka to think about her future. At first she didn't know what she wanted to do with her life. The days passed and she started thinking clearer. School was definitely her number one priority, and she decided to do the internet thing.

"Quit trippin', girl. You sure you want to do this?"

"Fo' real, are you crazy?" Victoria asked, smiling. "I can get paid doing the same thing only without having people touching me. It's a win-win situation."

"Alright then, I'm going to call Renee so we can get this shit crackin."

"What you mean 'we'?" Victoria asked.

"Quit trippin', girl. I know you don't think I'm a let you get all that money by yourself. Shit, I still wanna get paid too," Anna Marie said, smacking her lips.

"Fo' real, and what about the baby?' Victoria asked.

"What about it?" Anna Marie asked flatly. "I still got a few month before I get all fat. So while I'm perfect, I'm a get paid."

"Perfect my ass," Victoria said, laughing. "Your ass is as perfect as your cooking skills."

"Quit trippin', girl. I can cook," Anna Marie said, rolling her eyes.

"Fo' real, a bologna sandwich doesn't really count," Victoria said, laughing.

"Quit trippin', heifer," Anna Marie said, giving Victoria the middle finger.

The two women sat around Kenneth's living room, chitchatting with each other, reminiscing over the past. Victoria mentioned a story with Tameka in it. Anna Marie said, "You know I went to see that bitch the other day."

"Fo' real, what did she have to say about herself?" Victoria asked.

"Nothing," Anna Marie said disappointingly. "That ho acted like I was wrong. Then had the nerve to call me a traitor… Judas…"

"A traitor…? Judas…?" Victoria asked in surprise. "Fo' real, she's been fucking everything without a dick, and she calls you a traitor? Forget her trifling-ass. We better off anyway."

"Exactly," Anna Marie said, smiling. "It's time to look forward to the future, and get this other money."

Victoria laughed and said, "I hear you on that one."

When Tameka first fell out with Victoria, she thought she would see Victoria at work. When Victoria didn't show, Tameka got worried. She started going to work, hoping Victoria would be there. She wanted the two of them to have a talk. Tameka didn't care if Victoria slept with Kenneth, or even loved him for that matter.

She wanted Victoria back in her life. As long as Victoria was around her, Tameka felt she would eventually win her back. With each passing day, Tameka lost more hope on ever seeing Victoria again. This was threatening to drive her crazy.

A month had gone by since the three women fought. Tameka was starting to feel lonely. At first Porsha was able to hold Tameka's interest, but as of late Tameka wanted more. She wanted Victoria back and she was getting desperate.

Tameka thought Victoria was staying with Anna Marie. She spent three nights outside of Anna Marie's mom's house with high hopes. Victoria never showed. Tameka then spent three nights watching Tonya's apartment since the two were so close. Again she came up empty. Tameka knew Victoria had no family and assumed Victoria was living with Kenneth. The thought of Kenneth and Victoria sleeping in the same bed drove Tameka crazier. The more she thought about it, the more she was motivated to find Victoria.

Because of his past, finding out where Kenneth lived would be very difficult. Kenneth made a lot of money in the drug game. He never once got robbed. His success was due to him being guardedly secret. Pete sold weed to all of the big-time drug dealers and Tameka decided to enlist his help. Pete would do anything for his sister, but this request was something he didn't want any part of.

"I know you crazy, but are you that crazy?" Pete asked, rolling a blunt. "I can't go around asking where Big Ken live?"

"Why?" Tameka asked in a little girl voice.

Pete shook his head and said, "Because it could get me killed, that's why."

"I don't understand," Tameka said, looking at Pete. "You sell dro to all of the niggas making money. So you got the connect. All you gotta do is work the question into one of your conversations. I'm sure somebody knows where he lives."

"It's not that simple," Pete said, lighting the blunt. "We just got into it with the nigga last month, and here I am asking where he lives. That don't look too good. A muthafucka gon' think I'm trying to get some get-back."

"So…?" Tameka asked.

"So… A muthafucka would tell him or J.T. to stay in good grace with 'em niggas," Pete said, passing the blunt toTameka. "I sell weed. So, I'm a lil' nigga… Them nigga's some heavyweights. You understand?"

"I'm sure you can ask somebody. I know you got a couple of niggas you can trust," Tameka said, puffing on the blunt.

"Why don't you let Victoria do her thing, and you do yours?" Pete asked.

Tameka blew out the smoke and said, "I can't do me. She is me."

Pete reached for the blunt and said, "That's deep. Especially since you were running around here fucking everybody we hired."

"Having sex does not equate to making love," Tameka said, leaning back in her chair. "I can fuck any girl I want, but I can only make love to Victoria."

"Don't get your hopes up, but I'll see what I can do," Pete said, passing the blunt to Tameka. "You still need to keep digging on your own."

Tameka took the blunt from Pete and said, "You can bet on it."

One week later, Tameka still didn't have a clue as to where Kenneth lived. Although Pete told her he would help, his actions were showing different. Tameka knew it would be up to her to ask questions, and do the searching. She knew just where to start.

Tameka, Tonya and Bambi were changing into their thong sets when Tameka said, "Tonya, are you picking up weight because that ass of yours is getting fat."

"Don't be looking at my ass," Tonya said, turning around. "You know I don't even get down like that."

"Like what?" Tameka asked, standing.

Bambi slammed her locker closed and said, "I'll see y'all on the floor."

Tameka walked within two feet of Tonya and stopped. She stared at her and said, "You don't get down like what?"

Tonya took a couple steps back and said, "Look, it ain't even that important. I'm about to hit the floor too."

Tonya took two steps and Tameka grabbed her by the arm. She said,

"Hold up. I ain't done talking to you."

Tonya snatched her arm away from Tameka and said, "You ain't got to be grabbing me like that. What you want?"

Tameka became serious and said, "I know you still see Victoria and I know you still talk to her. I just want to know where she's staying, that's all."

Tonya looked at the floor. She said, "I don't know."

Tameka pushed Tonya back against the lockers and put her finger on Tonya's forehead.

"You might as well tell me now. Because one way or another, I'm a get it out of you."

"I don't know anything," Tonya said, trying to push Tameka away. "She calls me and we meet at different places. I don't know where she's staying."

"Oh, you know," Tameka said, running her fingers across Tonya's breast. "All you got to do is tell me where Kenneth lives and this will all be over."

"Stop," Tonya said, moving Tameka's hand. "I told you, I don't know anything."

"Alright but this one's on you," Tameka said and stuck her hand inside Tonya's thong so fast Tonya didn't know what was happening. "You like that, don't you?" Tameka asked, sliding one of her fingers inside of Tonya's pussy.

Tonya pushed Tameka with all of her might and said, "You crazy bitch. If you ever do that shit again, I'm a kill yo ass."

Tameka smiled and licked her finger. She said, "Finger licking good…"

Tonya opened her locker. She grabbed her clothes and purse. Staring at Tameka with a sick look, she said, "I quit." She stormed pass Tameka.

"Go ahead, bitch. Yo ass was in the way anyway!" Tameka shouted.

Tameka was feeling herself losing it. She had to pull herself together quickly. If she didn't, she knew something bad was going to happen.

Porsha thought she was falling in love with Tameka. She caught Tameka trying to fuck the newest member of the Cash Money Queens. Tameka's insensitiveness reminded Porsha how much of a parasite Tameka really was. Porsha knew no matter what she did, Tameka wouldn't hurt like she had, but

Porsha was going to have fun trying anyway.

Victoria and Anna Marie's departure left, Tameka to put Pete in charge of closing up. She didn't want to be in the club anymore than she had to. Pete would hurry the women through a quick shower so that he could leave.

The women became accustomed to Pete rushing them and started taking five minute showers just to avoid hearing his mouth. On this particular night, Pete heard the showers still running thirty minutes after the club was closed. When Pete went in the back he stood frozen, Barbie and Porsha were in a sixty-nine position, busy eating out each other.

Porsha raised her head from Barbie's pussy and said, "You wanna join us?"

"Nah, I wanna watch," Pete said, taking a seat on the bench.

"Suit yourself, but know that you can join us at anytime," Porsha said with a devious smile.

Pete continued sitting on the bench and watching. Barbie was lying on the floor while Porsha was positioned over her. Barbie's tongue kept slowly sliding in and out of Porsha's pussy. Barbie looked like she was enjoying herself but Pete thought Porsha wasn't. Porsha was busy sliding two of her fingers in and out of Barbie's pussy while sucking on Barbie's clit. Although Porsha was pleasuring Barbie she kept looking over at Pete whose dick was rock hard.

"Fuck it!" Pete said, hurrying out of his clothes. "Tameka wouldn't mind no way."

Pete walked over to the naked women and without warning, slid his dick over Barbie's tongue and buried it deep inside Porsha's pussy.

"What the hell is you doing?" Barbie asked angrily.

"Shut up and suck my nuts, lick my ass or something," Pete said, driving his dick in and out of Porsha's hot opening.

Barbie did just that. She dropped her attitude and started sucking Pete's balls. At first Barbie had a hard time keeping his nuts in her mouth, but once Pete slowed down, the three of them had the perfect rhythm. Pete drove his dick slowly in and out of Porsha's pussy.

"Oh yes, Pete. I been wanting to be fucked like that, nice and slow," Porsha moaned.

She continued sucking and finger-fucking Barbie. Barbie rotated from sucking Pete's balls to licking his butt cheeks. When Barbie would lick Pete's ass cheeks she cupped his balls in one of her hands and massaged them. Barbie tried to lick Porsha's clit and instead lick Pete's dick.

"Ah shit!" Pete moaned.

Seeing how Pete reacted to the stimulation of her tongue, Barbie continued to lick Pete's dick as it went in and came out of Porsha's gaping, running with juice.

"Oh yes! I'm—oh, oh, oh cumming!" Porsha screamed.

"Me too," Pete said, losing control. Pete grabbed Porsha by her hips and sped up the pace. Driving his manhood in and out of Porsha's pussy real fast, she was unable to give Barbie pleasure. Pete's strokes were not only fast, but forceful. Porsha could tell Pete was enjoying himself especially when Pete started smacking her on her ass.

"That's right, give it to me, daddy. Give it to me," Porsha said, erupting.

Not even a minute later Porsha and Barbie heard Pete groaned, "Ooh, this some good, good pussy!"

The two women laughed at Pete then Barbie said, "Y'all got y'all shits off, but what about me?"

Pete walked under the shower head and said, "Don't worry. I got you next just let me get some of this sweat off my face."

Barbie walked behind Pete and wrapped her arms around his waist, grabbing his dick with her right hand.

"Let me help you with this big ol' thang," she said and slowly started stroking Pete's dick.

Pete's manhood went from being soft to semi-hard. Porsha walked in front of Pete and dropped to her knees.

"Let me help y'all out," she said, taking every bit of Pete's semi-hard dick into her warm mouth.

"Ah shit," Pete moaned. "That's what I'm talking about right there.

Ooh, don't stop."

Porsha didn't. After thirty seconds of lip service Pete was hard as ever, but Porsha kept sucking.

"Hey, hey, it's my turn. Remember?" Barbie said, pulling Pete away from Porsha's lips.

Barbie didn't want the water distracting her. She led Pete to a dry place and laid him down. Barbie grabbed Pete's dick and lowered herself down on it. Inch by inch Pete's dick disappeared inside Barbie's pussy. There was nothing left. Barbie had all nine inches of his dick inside her. She sat there enjoying the feel of it. When Pete started rubbing Barbie's ass, she slowly began to move.

Barbie was doing her thing. She was being careful not to break the rhythm she and Pete found. Porsha was going to let Pete and Barbie enjoy the sex, but after sucking Pete's dick, Porsha was right back to being horny again. She walked over to where they were and squatted over Pete's face.

"You know you want to taste me."

"Damn right," Pete said, grabbing Porsha's hip and pulling her closer to him. As soon as Pete stuck his tongue in Porsha's pussy, he immediately knew why Tameka dealt with her. Porsha's pussy was pleasing to Pete's palate. It showed when he gripped Porsha's thighs harder and dug his mouth even deeper inside, tasting her moisture.

Meanwhile, Barbie was starting to pick up the pace. Porsha intentionally positioned herself facing Barbie. Barbie slid her pussy up and down on Pete's dick. Porsha reached out and grabbed Barbie's breasts. Barbie smiled and started playing with her clit. She continued to bounce up and down on Pete's dick.

"Oh, oh, oh man yes! Oh!" Barbie screamed out as she and Pete exploded together.

"Ooh yes!" Porsha screamed when she felt an eruption.

Juices were dripping down her legs, and off Pete's chin. The three individuals kicked back, and smoked two blunts. Their sex episode was so nice that they started making plans to get together again.

CHAPTER EIGHTEEN

It was the middle of March 2002. Ass By The Pound's clientele was once again declining. In the past the police were the reason for the club's financial woes but this time it was the club's fault. Customers had grown tired of having to share the five remaining women with each other. The club needed more dancers and the customers voiced their complaints to Tameka and Pete.

He hoped the complaints would motivate Tameka out of her depression. This could cause her to go searching for some new talent. He was wrong. Tameka paid the customers no mind and continued doing nothing.

The customers wanted to stay faithful to Ass By The Pound. Their complaints went ignored and some of them started looking elsewhere for their entertainment. No new clubs had opened. Pete thought the customers went to The Lady Fox to see Desire. Pete had no idea on how to bring the customers back. He had no clue on what his next move should be. Ultimately, Pete decided to do nothing, hoping Tameka would come back around before all of their customers left.

Ass By The Pound was unusually full the last Friday in March. There were a lot of new faces in the club which caused the women to think their days of struggling were over. The new customers stayed in groups of fours which brought unwanted attention to the men. The men were not dressed stylish so the dancers couldn't tell if they had money. They quickly learned who the men were and what they were about once they approached them.

"Come here, shorty," a big, dark brown skinned man said. "Let me holla at you for a minute."

Porsha could tell from the man's southern accent that he wasn't from Gary.

"Where you from?" she asked, smiling.

"I'm from Decatur, Georgia," the man answered with a smile. "My name is Bookie. What's yours?"

"My name is Porsha and what y'all doing all the way up here?"

"We heard about this club from my cousin. He said it was off the chain," Bookie said, looking around the place. "But it looks dead in here to me."

"Yeah, that's because the three owners fell out, and some of the other dancers quit," Porsha said then smiled. "But the faithful is still up in here to please."

Bookie sat his drink down and said, "I know you don't think I came all this way to watch y'all dance."

"So why did you come?" Porsha asked with curiosity.

"Why don't you have a seat? I came to offer some of y'all a job," Bookie said, signaling for one of his men to get up so Porsha could sit down.

Porsha sat down and listened to Bookie's sales pitch. It didn't take Porsha long to discover what Bookie's job was.

"Porno...?" Porsha asked in surprise. "You want me to do porno? Boy, are you crazy?"

Bookie remained straight faced. "Look around you, this shit ain't gone last too much longer and then what are you gonna do?"

"I'm a find me another job at another club." Porsha said defiantly.

Bookie laughed, shaking his head and said, "So you wanna shake yo ass for the next ten to fifteen years, and still have nothing to show for it?" Bookie leaned on the table. "I'm offering you a chance of a lifetime. If you join my team you could be making six figures a year."

"Doing what?" Porsha asked anxiously.

"The same shit you do probably every day," Bookie said flatly. "Look, I'm a business man, not a pimp. Nothing will be forced on you. You're an adult and you can do what you wanna," Bookie said, sliding something across the table to Porsha. "Here's my business card. I'm only going to be down here two more days, after that I'm gone."

Porsha examined Bookie's business card and said, "I'm going to do a little research, and get back at you."

"You do that," Bookie said, standing and showing his full six-four, two hundred and thirty pound frame. "And see if some of the other women are interested too."

"I most certainly will," Porsha said, putting Bookie's card away.

Things were starting to look bad for Tonya. It had been one month since she quit her job at the club and now she was regretting it. Of all the dancers who had worked at the club, Tonya made the least amount of money. The other women were making two and three thousand dollars a night, Tonya was struggling to make one thousand. Despite her financial shortcomings, Tonya still managed to move her and her little sister, Alisa, into a nice apartment complex. While Tonya had thousands saved in the bank, she wasn't trying to spend too much of it on monthly expenses. Tonya went on job interviews in search of a respectable job, but after a couple days of rejection, Tonya decided it was time to seek advice from her big sister.

"Hey there gorgeous," Victoria said, opening Kenneth's front door. "Come give your auntie a hug."

Alisa gave Victoria a hug and said, "Auntie Victoria, Tonya won't let me play baseball at Tolleston Park."

Tonya walked in the door and said, "That girl acts more like a boy with each passing day. I don't know what I'm a do with her."

Victoria laughed, shutting the door and said, "She'll be all right."

"Wow Auntie Victoria, is this your house?" Alisa asked, looking around the living room.

"No sweetie," Victoria said, sitting down on the sofa. "This is a friend of mine's house."

"Dang, he must be paid," Alisa said, turning the big screen television to the Cartoon Network.

Victoria and Tonya both laughed. Tonya sat on the sofa and Victoria could immediately tell something was bothering her.

"So what brings you out here, the club wearing you out?"

Tonya shook her head and said, "Nah, the club's not the problem anymore because I quit."

"Fo' real…?" Victoria asked in surprise. "When did this happen?"

"Five weeks ago," Alisa blurted.

"Alisa, what have I told you about getting in grown people's conversations?"

Alisa turned around and faced Tonya. She said, "It's not polite to get in other people's conversations if it's not my business."

Tonya's worried expression turned to one of disgust. Staring at her younger sister, she said, "I don't know what I'm going to do with her."

"She'll be all right," Victoria said, winking at Alisa. "Fo' real, we're all family up in here." Victoria got up from the couch and sat on the sofa next to Tonya. "Fo' real, Alisa's not the problem. Why don't you tell me what's really bothering you?"

"I'm frustrated because I can't find another job, a better job," Tonya said, hanging her head.

"Fo' real, girl, that's all? You ain't got to be worried about no job. I got you," Victoria said, smacking her lips.

"Got me how?" Tonya asked with curiosity.

"Come with me," Victoria said, standing.

Tonya and Victoria went into the kitchen. Once the two women were privately seated at the kitchen table, Victoria spoke.

"I'm in the process of starting an Internet company."

"An Internet company...?" Tonya asked, confused. "What kind of Internet company gon' get us paid?"

"Stripping," Victoria said and smiled. "Fo' real, we'll be doing the same thing we did at the club only in the privacy of an apartment we'll be renting."

"And people gon' pay us for that?" Tonya asked still confused.

"Yeah silly," Victoria said, laughing. "I guess it's the new thing. I'm still getting everything set up, but you're more than welcome to join us."

"Us...?" Tonya asked in surprise. "I thought you said it was only you."

Victoria hit herself upside her head. She said, "Fo' real, my fault. Anna Marie is my partner. I'm sure she wouldn't mind one more partner. So what do you say?"

"I'm in," Tonya said happily.

Porsha did her research and found out Bookie was a legitimate businessman. According to Porsha's source, Bookie started out making and selling videos of different strip clubs. Once he made a name for himself, he produced a porno film. Porsha's source reported that the movie caused a stir, but wasn't good. He, however, sold enough to increase the quality of his next movie. The second movie not only made Bookie an instant success, it also helped propel him into the magazine business. He also owned a triple X-rated magazine. Porsha was more than satisfied with the information she received.

She shared the information with the other women. Barbie and Bambi told her they would join, if the dollars were right. Porsha placed the call and the three women sat in Porsha's apartment waiting on Bookie to show up.

Victoria was exhausted. She had spent the entire day cleaning Kenneth's five bedrooms, three bathrooms, and two-kitchen house. The place was now spotless. Victoria prepared a nice dinner for her and Kenneth. While Victoria was waiting on Kenneth she laid on the couch watching a movie on the Lifetime channel. Twenty minutes into the movie, Victoria fell asleep and thirty minutes into her sleep Victoria's nightmare began.

She was seven year-old, lying in her bed asleep. A man awoke her out of her sleep by rubbing her leg. The young Victoria couldn't see the man's face but she wasn't frightened by him. There was something familiar about the man. A sleepy eye Victoria asked, "What's wrong?"

The man continued to rub Victoria's leg and said, "Nothing. I just wanted to talk to you. Can I talk to you?"

"Yes," the young Victoria answered.

The man continued to rub Victoria's leg. Each time he would move his hand up a little closer to Victoria's crotch.

"You know I've been watching you. And you've been a good little girl. Since you've been so good I have something for you," the man said, taking his free hand and sticking it in his back pants pocket. He would pull out a rainbow lollipop and said, "For you." He handed it to her.

Victoria took the sucker and said, "Thank you."

The man's hand finally made it to Victoria's panties. She squirmed when she felt the man's finger outside her opening.

"Everything's going to be all right," the man said, prying one of his fingers inside Victoria's small opening.

"It hurts," the young Victoria said, crying.

The man took his finger out of Victoria and placed it to his lip. He said, "Shush. It's going to be all right." The man pulled down his pants. "I have another lollipop for you sweetie," he offered.

"Where is it?" the young Victoria asked.

"Right here," the man said, pointing to his dick. "All you have to do is put your mouth around it and suck on it."

"No," the young Victoria said shaking her head.

"Come on sweetie, it's all right."

"No, I don't want to," the young Victoria said. The man pulled up his pants and started walking out of the room. "Daddy, are you mad at me?"

"No sweetheart, daddy's fine," her father said, walking out the room. Victoria awoke from her dream crying.

Bookie stood in Porsha's living room surrounded by Porsha, Bambi and Barbie. The women were busy asking him questions like they were interviewing him.

"Like I said before, the amount of money y'all make will depend on y'all. If y'all do one or two movies a year then y'all will see little money. If y'all do five to ten movies a year then y'all will see a lot of money."

"I don't think I can do anal on camera," Bambi said, looked around the room. "That shit be hurting. And I know I be making some fucked up faces."

Bookie laughed and said, "It can't be that bad. But on the real that's where the money at. Anal sex is real big right now, and if you want we'll give you a little dick muthafucka. As y'all will come to see, I'm a very fair boss."

"I can see that already," Barbie said in a flirtatious way. "I'm sure it's going to be a pleasure working for you."

Porsha rolled her eyes at Barbie and said, "I can have ya'll first movie setup in two months. That will give y'all enough time to get everything in order here. But y'all will have to be in Decatur in six weeks time."

"Six weeks it is," Porsha said, shaking Bookie's hand.

Kenneth came home to find Victoria balled up on the couch she was crying.

"What's wrong baby?" Kenneth asked, rushing to her side.

Victoria wrapped her arms around Kenneth's neck and said, "Just hold me."

Kenneth held Victoria in his arms. Caressing her face, he said, "I got you baby. I got you."

He consoled Victoria for over an hour. Once all Victoria's tears were out the way, she told Kenneth about her dreams. Kenneth listened in disbelief. She shared the horrific details with him. Victoria was finished and the two sat in silence for an eternity. Kenneth left to run hot bath for her. Victoria sat in the tub and he massaged her temples.

Kenneth's touch was so loving and comforting that all of Victoria's confusion seemed to melt away. Victoria saw everything clearly. She began to plan a seduction. Victoria was done with her bath she looked up at Kenneth.

"You know what will make me feel even better?"

"No," Kenneth said, shakink his head.

"Some strawberry éclairs from Izzy's…"

"Right now…?" Kenneth asked, surprised.

"Yes baby, please," Victoria said in her softest voice.

"Alright," Kenneth said as he stood up. "I'll be back as soon as possible."

Kenneth kissed Victoria on her forehead and left. Victoria heard the front door closed and jumped out of the tub. She knew the truth about her nightmare and wasn't going to let her fear of men hold her back anymore.

Victoria went around the bedroom arranging everything. By the time Kenneth made it back to his house, Victoria was done. He walked into the bedroom and froze. Candles were lit all around the bedroom and Sade played softly in the background. Victoria was naked in his bed. Kenneth regained his composure and walked to the bed.

"Victoria, Victoria," he said.

She heard him, but Victoria didn't respond. She remained lying still on the bed.

"Victoria, are you asleep?" Kenneth asked, getting closer to the bed.

She waited until Kenneth was standing directly above her, before opening her eyes.

"Come here," she said, pulling him down on the bed. "Fo' real, tonight's your lucky night."

"Oh yeah...?" Kenneth asked, smiling. "And why is that?"

"Because tonight, I want you to make love to me," Victoria said, looking deep into Kenneth's eyes.

"Are you sure?" Kenneth asked. He was shocked.

"Positive," Victoria said, pulling Kenneth on top of her.

He undressed and slid back on top of Victoria giving her a long, passionate tongue kiss. Kenneth pulled his tongue out of Victoria's mouth and started running it around her lips. He began licking Victoria on her neck, following each lick with a suck and soft kiss. By the time Kenneth made it to Victoria's breasts, her nipples were fully erect and pointing straight out.

Kenneth massage Victoria's breast while running his tongue up and down Victoria's stomach. Returning to her breast, his tongue flicked at Victoria's nipples. Taking as much of her breast as he could into his mouth, Kenneth sucked Victoria's breasts. His main focus was reaching Victoria's love box. He wanted so badly to taste her, and continued running his tongue downward until he hit the jackpot.

Victoria's pussy was so wet it looked like she had an orgasm. She went crazy when Kenneth stuck his tongue inside her. Victoria grabbed Kenneth by his head, holding him at her pussy. Without missing a beat, he wrapped his tongue over Victoria's clit and slid one of his fingers inside her opening.

Kenneth's finger worked its way in and out of Victoria's pussy. Kenneth soon replaced his finger with his tongue. This time when Kenneth stuck his tongue inside Victoria's pussy he massaged her clit with his thumb. It caused Victoria to start humping Kenneth's face. Ten seconds later, Victoria shook uncontrollably and exploded.

"Oh, ah, Kenneth," she sang, feeling the eruption below her navel.

He waited for Victoria to stop shaking before wrapping his mouth around her clit and sucking it. His sucks were powerful. When he slid his finger inside of her, Victoria had another orgasm. Kenneth inched his way back up to Victoria's lips, kissing her body all the way back up. He kissed her lips long and hard. Kenneth grabbed his dick and slid it inside of Victoria. Kissing her even harder, he slid two more inches inside. Victoria started panting when Kenneth had seven inches inside of her.

"Are you all right?" Kenneth asked.

"You just keep going," Victoria sighed, taking a deep breath.

Victoria's pussy was getting pounded and Kenneth was careful not to exceed seven inches. He kept sliding his dick until the last two inches inside of her. Kenneth held it there then he started slowly moving his dick in and out of Victoria's wet pussy. Slow and steady Kenneth went until Victoria started bucking back. She rolled Kenneth on his back and took control. After a few awkward minutes, Victoria found her stride and rode Kenneth to ecstasy.

CHAPTER NINETEEN

It had been two weeks since Victoria discovered the truth about her nightmares. In those two weeks, Victoria and Kenneth had been making love any and everywhere they could. Victoria didn't want to deal with the reality of her father sexually abusing her. She divided her time between putting the finishing touches on their internet company, and making love to Kenneth. She loved making love to Kenneth, but business came first. Anna Marie and J.T. were coming back to town today.

"How was your trip?" Victoria asked, opening the front door.

"Quit trippin', girl. It was cool. But it would have been better if I had my best friend there to kick it with when J.T. was handling his business. You know you and Kenneth could have come," Anna Marie announced, walking inside.

"Uh, uh, you know Kenneth don't want to put himself nowhere around his old lifestyle," Victoria said, shaking her head.

"Hold up," Anna Marie said, looking Victoria up and down. "Something's different about you. What you been around here doing?"

"Nothing," Victoria said, blushing.

"Quit trippin', no you didn't, you little heifer," Anna Marie said, smiling. "You finally got some dick, huh?"

"Fo' real, shut up. I didn't get no dick. For your information I made love," Victoria said, but couldn't stop smiling.

"Quit trippin', girl. My sister got her cherry popped. It's about time. I wish I could drink to it but you know," she said, pointing at her belly.

"Look at you," Victoria said, rubbing Anna Marie's stomach. "Fo' real you starting to show…"

"Quit trippin', girl," Anna Marie said, rolling her eyes. "I just bought this outfit last week. And I can barely fit it now."

"Fo' real, come on now, you know your ass is about to be bigger than Bertha's," Victoria said, laughing.

"Fuck you cow!" Anna Marie said, smiling.

The two women spent the rest of the afternoon going over the particulars involved with their internet company.

Three months had flown by since Victoria left Tameka. She was still trying to find out where Kenneth lived. Tameka felt if she explained everything to Victoria then she could win her back. Tameka stayed focused on finding Victoria, but the world around her was steadily crumbling.

Not only was she losing money at the club, she also quit her job at the grocery store because of personal hygiene problems. Tameka went from one hundred and thirty-five pounds to one hundred and seventy pounds. She quit getting her hair done, and even smelled like stale pussy on some occasions. Pete hated seeing what was becoming of Tameka, but each time he tried talking to her, his words fell on deaf ears.

Ass By The Pound was no longer on the lips of the big-time drug dealers. The club's hype had been stolen by a new club, Top Notch Hoes. The owner not only stole Tameka's customers, but also stole her idea of operating illegally. Since Top Notch Hoes wasn't licensed, the dancers could do and show whatever they wanted. While Top Notch Hoes seemed like it was the spot to be in Ass By The Pound was slowly becoming a thing of the past.

Porsha, Bambi and Barbie were leaving in less than two weeks. Pete had to make something happen. He knew Angel couldn't carry the club's load by herself. Pete reluctantly went out searching for new dancers. Pete decided that since he was about to do something he didn't want to do, he would drag Tameka with him to each and every club.

While Anna Marie was away with J.T., Victoria handled her business. She rented an apartment in Gary's Miller area. It was to be the home of their internet company, Butt Naked Sistas.com. Victoria, with the help of Tonya also furnished the apartment with two canopy beds, three cameras and one computer. She listed their website on three of the biggest search engines she could find, and also set up Paypal account so they could get paid.

Victoria wanted worldwide exposure and contacted the two biggest rap magazines for advertisement. Anna Marie was back and joined forces with Tonya and Victoria to do the photo shoot for their ads.

Staying true to himself, Pete dragged Tameka to every club he visited. While Tameka seemed uninterested, Pete talked to a lot of potential dancers and got their numbers. It seemed like each club Pete, Tameka, Boo Rock, O.J. and Angel visited, Pete heard the same question popping up.

"Are y'all from Top Notch Hoes?"

Each time Tameka heard the question, she smiled and said nothing. She remembered when the question used to be, "Are y'all from Ass By The Pound?"

Pete did a little research and found out the club operated like Ass By The Pound. Top Notch Hoes wasn't licensed, was started by a stripper, opened only on Friday, Saturday and Sunday and more importantly, there were no rules. Once he had all the facts, Pete decided to make the trip to Top Notch Hoes. It seemed like the owner was out to purposely destroy Ass By The Pound.

The last Friday in April, Pete closed the club and allowed the Ass By The Pound crew to check out the competition. Pete wanted to meet the person who was hell-bent on destroying them. They walked in Top Notch Hoes and it was as if they had just walked into Ass By The Pound. The two clubs were identical in every way.

"This is bullshit," Boo Rock said, glancing around the club. "They stole our style."

"Yeah, but who the fuck is stealing our style?" Pete asked, nodding his head.

"Correction," Angel said, watching a dancer flirt with a customer. "Stole our style…"

The place was jam packed. There were more customers than there were chairs. Pete looked around the club and saw all their former patrons. He even saw some of their new ones. Pete shook his head in disbelief.

"I can't believe that these niggas would leave us for a knockoff."

"Believe it," a voice said from behind them. The whole group turned around and stared in amazement. "What's wrong, cat got y'all tongue?"

"It's this traitor-ass-bitch!" Tameka said with a scowl on her face. "After everything I did for yo ass you betray me like this?"

"Bitch, shut the fuck up. I could have had yo ass put in jail for rape," Renee said matter-of-factly.

"Rape…?" Angel asked in surprise. "What she mean rape?"

"She just talking. I ain't gotta rape nothing," Tameka said, keeping her eyes fixed on Renee.

"Look at you," Renee said, laughing. "You fat, smelly and obviously miserable… You is a joke!"

"Fuck you bitch!" Tameka responded.

"You already did that," Renee said, walking away. "Now if y'all will excuse me, I have a club to run."

"But why you steal our style?" O.J. asked.

"To destroy Tameka," Renee said, looking directly at Tameka. "It seems like all of us that left y'all tired-ass club is doing good for themselves."

"All of who?" Tameka asked.

"After I told Victoria about all your sexcapades, I gave her the game on getting some money legally," Renee smiled.

"You bitch!" Tameka said, charging at Renee.

Renee quickly ran behind one of her security guards and said, "Get this smelly bitch out of my club."

Tameka looked at the six-six, three hundred pound man and said, "This ain't over bitch." Tameka walked back over to her group and they all left.

With the start of their internet company Victoria appeared stressed out now more than ever. Butt Naked Sistas.com only played a minor role in the sudden rise in Victoria's stress level. Her court date from the mall incident was only two weeks away, and final exams were only days away.

In the past Victoria would become unbearable around finals, but that wasn't the case this semester. Instead of isolating herself away from everyone, Victoria did the opposite. She was reaching out to everyone. No one could figure out the change in Victoria's actions, but it soon became clear.

The week of final exams was a blur to her. Victoria was confident she passed all of her exams, but her mind was still preoccupied with her court case. Two days before Victoria was scheduled to go to court, her lawyer contacted her with a plea agreement. Victoria would plead guilty to a misdemeanor assault in exchange for three years probation. She didn't want to accept the plea without talking to Anna Marie first. Victoria told her lawyer that she would think about it and call him back with her decision.

When she hung up the phone, Victoria screamed at the top of her lungs from excitement. She thought there would be actual jail time. After hearing the good news from her lawyer, Victoria could now focus on her future. The threat of jail would finally be over. She heard the phone ringing.

"Hello," Victoria said, picking up the receiver.

"Quit trippin', heifer," Anna Marie said.

"Fo' real, I was just about to call you," Victoria said, plopping down on the sofa. "I just got off the phone with the lawyer."

"Me too," Anna Marie said, still sounding happy. "They offered me five years probation."

"That's good," Victoria said happily. "They're offering me three years."

Anna Marie's tone became serious when she said, "My lawyer said I only got probation because I'm pregnant, otherwise I would be joining Tameka in a cell."

"What?" Victoria said surprised.

"Yeah, my lawyer said her deal is for two years jail time. Oh well," Anna Marie said in a carefree manner.

"Fo' real, that's messed up," Victoria said sympathetically.

Anna Marie's voice rose when she said, "Quit trippin', girl. She done did it to herself. She on her own, we gotta look out for us."

"You're right," Victoria said. Her heart was hurting for Tameka.

Tameka's life had changed dramatically over the past three weeks, and it was due to her encounter with Renee. After Tameka left Top Notch Hoes that night, she made up her mind to regain control of her life. Tameka went on a diet and started exercising twice a day. In three weeks she lost fifteen pounds, and started taking pride in her appearance again. She vowed to restore Ass By The Pound to its glory, but after talking to her lawyer she started making other plans.

Tameka, Victoria and Anna Marie sat in court room waiting on the judge to come out. Tameka sat one row behind Victoria, Kenneth, J.T. and Anna Marie. She kept her eyes fixed on Victoria. All the while she was thinking about how good Victoria looked. The judge came out and the proceedings began.

One by one people were called in front of the judge. Victoria was the first from their group to be in front of the judge, relating her version of the mall incident. The judge accepted her version and granted her plea.

Tameka was the next one to go in front of the judge. The judge also accepted her plea and let her remain free until her sentencing date, set for three weeks away. After Tameka was finished she walked out of the courtroom without even looking at Victoria and Anna Marie.

Anna Marie was the last person in the courtroom to see the judge. No one knew why until Anna Marie went before him, and he started talking. He told her she was lucky to be pregnant. He would have sent her to jail also. Anna Marie held her tongue in check and the four of them left the courtroom happy. Tameka was in the parking lot waiting.

Tameka followed Kenneth all the way to his house. She now had Victoria's location, but still lacked the words to say to her. Tameka decided to wait until she came up with the right words to say before approaching Victoria. Although Tameka was happy she knew where Victoria lived, she was very angry about having to go to jail. It showed in her attitude.

With Tameka back to her old self, Ass By The Pound's clientele was slowly picking up. Not only was Tameka not going to let the club fail, but she was determined to beat Renee at her own game by restoring Ass By The Pound to its number one spot. To help her with her cause and to replace Porsha, Barbie and Bambi, Tameka hired three beautiful new dancers and was still searching for two more. This all took place before Tameka went to court.

With less than three weeks of freedom left, Tameka was all about stacking her money. She had no plans of getting out of jail and returning to stripping. In hopes of getting more money, Tameka now did two stage routines instead of one.

It was late Friday night and Tameka was dead tired. She had just finished her second stage routine. On her way to the dressing room, a man grabbed her by the arm.

"Excuse me, but can I get a lap dance?" the man asked, holding out a twenty dollar bill.

Tameka looked at the twenty, chuckled and said, "I'm sorry, baby, but I'm tired and it's going to take more than twenty dollars to get me un-tired."

The man pulled out another twenty and said, "Now what's up?"

Tameka could see the man was desperate, but she was too exhausted to dance anymore and said, "I would, but I'm all sweaty. Plus I'm really tired. Lemme go shower."

"No!" the man shouted. "I want you to stay sweaty."

Tameka turned up her nose and said, "I don't do perverts." She began to walk off. "Get one of these other bitches to get yo kicks off of."

The man grabbed Tameka by her arm again. He said, "Bitch, you see this?" He flashed a police badge. "I can shut this house down if I want to." He put the badge away and flashed Tameka a smile then said, "Now you wanna give me that dance?"

Tameka snatched her arm away from the man. "Nigga please, I done seen fake badges before. Get the fuck outta my face!"

The man grabbed Tameka by her shoulders and Tameka responded with a knee to his groin. "Stupid pervert! Get off of me!"

"You bitch!" he said, groaning.

"Pete!" Tameka screamed. Pete made it over to her and Tameka pointed at the man. She angrily said, "Get this nigga out of here before I catch another case."

"Come on playa, it's time for you to go," Pete said, helping the man to his feet.

"I'm a kill you!" the man said when he was on his feet.

Tameka jumped back and Pete grabbed the man by his shirt and slammed him to the ground.

"I told yo ass it was time to go," Pete said, stomping away at the man. "I tried to be peaceful, but you wouldn't let me."

"That's enough. That's enough," Boo Rock said, pulling Pete away from the man.

"Fuck that shit! Get his ass outta here before I kill him," Pete said, amped up.

O.J. and Boo Rock were dragging the man out of the club and he said, "I'm close this bitch down tomorrow."

Saturday came and Tameka came up with a new way to eliminate Top Notch Hoes. She had a simple, but dangerous plan. Tameka had no clue on how she was going to carry out her plan or even if she should tell Pete. The only thing she knew was after tonight Ass By The Pound would be jammed pack every night since the club would now be open seven days a week. While Tameka was planning her attack on Top Notch Hoes, Officer Daniels was planning his attack on Ass By The Pound.

Tameka watched Renee, four women and two men go inside Top Notch Hoes around seven o'clock. Since it was too early to open the club Tameka figured they were setting up for the night's show. Tameka sat in her car hoping Renee stole their food ritual along with all the other ideas she stole from Ass By The Pound. If Renee did steal the food ritual it meant they would be coming out of the club any minute to go get something to eat. Tameka lit a blunt and told herself whether they leave or not, Top Notch Hoes was getting burned to the ground that night.

Around eight thirty Renee walked out the club with her co-workers right behind her. The group got into three different cars and left. Tameka didn't know if Renee had seen her car so she waited five extra minutes before she got out of her car, and walked over to the club carrying two five gallon gasoline cans.

Entering the club was no problem since Tameka was taught how to pick door locks before she was taught how to drive. Once inside she wasn't worried about perfection, her only concern was not getting caught. Tameka poured gasoline on any and every thing that would burn. In three minutes she was standing in the doorway lighting the matches. Tameka threw the matches inside Top Notch Hoes and walked away.

It didn't take long for the fire to spread throughout the entire club. Tameka wanted to see Renee's expression but knew she had to go get her alibi tight. Renee and her co-workers returned to see the club burning.

"This some bullshit," Renee said, jumping out of her car. "I know that bitch did this!"

"You want us to call the fire department?" one of the dancers asked.

"For what…?" Renee asked testily. "Do you see what I see? Ain't shit to save."

One of Renee's bouncers walked up to her and said, "Since they shut us down, we should go shut they ass down."

"You right," Renee said, nodding her head. "Come on, let's go."

After Tameka left Top Notch Hoes she made a detour. She was reeking from the smell of gasoline. It was so strong that she had to drive with all four of her car windows down. Although everyone would think Tameka was involved in the burning down of Top Notch Hoes, she didn't want to give any proof. Tameka decided to go back home, take a shower, and change her clothes.

Pete was standing at the front door when Renee and co-workers arrived at Ass By The Pound. The group tried storming pass Pete.

"Whoa, wait a minute," Pete said, extending his arms to stop them. "What the fuck is y'all doing here?"

"Get out the way, Pete," Renee said, her eyes searching the club. "Where that bitch at?"

"Which bitch you talking about?" Pete asked.

Renee smacked her lips and said, "You know what bitch I'm talking about. Tameka."

"Why are you looking for my sister?" Pete asked.

"That bitch burned my club down," Renee said angrily. "Now tell me where she at?"

"Y'all gots to go," Pete said, motioning for O.J. and Boo Rock. "And Renee, you need to be careful about accusing innocent people."

"That bitch ain't innocent and you know it," Renee said, looking Pete dead in his eyes. "You know all the foul shit she be doing."

"Look Renee," Pete said getting irritated. "I ain't got time for yo shit. Y'all gots to get outta here!"

Before Renee could respond, a rush came from behind her.

"Everybody get on the muthfuckin ground! This a raid!" a police officer said as forty Gary Police Officers stormed the club.

Officer Daniels walked up to Pete smiled and said, "Remember me?" He dangled a pair of handcuffs in Pete's face. "Turn around and put your hands behind your back because yo black ass is going to jail."

"For what…?" Pete asked.

"Assaulting a police officer, dickhead," Officer Daniels said, trying to forcefully turn Pete around.

"This some bullshit," Pete said, pulling away from Officer Daniels. "Don't put yo fuckin' hands on me!"

"I got one resisting over her!" Officer Daniels shouted.

Six police officers rushed Pete. Before he knew it, Pete was face down on the ground. Pete looked up to find Officer Daniels smiling.

"Laugh now nigga! This shit ain't over!"

"Oh, there go another charge, threatening a police officer," Officer Daniels said, looking down at Pete. "You just don't know when to quit. Now where is the young lady that helped you assault me?"

"Fuck you, I ain't telling you shit!" Pete said.

"Suit yourself," Officer Daniels said, walking away. "If she's in here, I will find her."

Tameka was on her way to Ass By The Pound. She saw the police surrounding the club and kept on driving pass the club. She had no idea where she was going. What should her next move be? She thought with her hands on the wheel.

The only thing Tameka knew for sure was that she now was going to jail for two years. Tameka drove two hours before coming to a stop in front of Kenneth's house. She didn't know why she ended up there and didn't care. Tameka wanted to see Victoria. She got out the car and went to the front door.

"Who is it?" Victoria asked, walking to the door.

"Tameka…"

Victoria looked through the peephole.

"Fo' real, what are you doing here? How did you find me?"

"Victoria, please let me come in. We're grown and I'm not trying to do this behind a closed door."

"Do what?"

"Apologize," Tameka said softly.

Victoria folded her arms behind closed the front door and said, "I'm listening."

"I'm sorry," Tameka said, leaning against the screen door. "I was stupid. I let money change me. Before any of this, we were friends, best friends. I don't want to lose you as my friend."

"You did let that little money change you," Victoria said, opening the front door.

"I know, I know," Tameka said, teary eyed. "A lot of things happened to me that caused me to not get my priorities straight. And our friendship is one of those priorities."

Victoria unlocked the screen door and said, "Fo' real, having to do time will change a person."

"Please believe it," Tameka said, laughing.

Victoria locked the door after Tameka walked inside. She said, "That was some fucked up shit. You should've gotten probation like me and Anna Marie did."

"I got bigger problems than that," Tameka said, sitting down on the sofa.

"What's bigger than having to go to jail for two years?"

"That two years might have just turned into ten or twenty," Tameka said, shaking her head.

"What happened?" Victoria asked anxiously.

"It's a long story and I'm more concerned with what's been up with you," Tameka said, a half smile clinging to her lips. "So what's been up?"

Victoria was extremely happy, but didn't want to throw her happiness in Tameka's face.

"Nothing much, I've just been trying to maintain."

"And what's up with Kenneth? Are you two an item now?"

"I wouldn't say that," Victoria lied.

"C'mon Victoria, we grown, you trying to tell me y'all haven't slept together." Victoria didn't respond. "It's cool, I can take a hint," Tameka said, sounding disappointed.

"Let's not talk about Kenneth," Victoria said, standing up.

"So you want to talk about, us?" Tameka asked.

"No, not that either," Victoria said, shaking her head.

"Why... Why did you leave me?"

"Fo' real, I'm not gay."

Tameka was shocked at Victoria's response and said, "You not gay? Bitch, you let me eat yo pussy and you loved it."

"You know what...? Fo' real, I think it's time for you to leave."

"We not finished yet, bitch," Tameka said and grabbed Victoria by the arm. "Did you fuck him?"

"Let me go," Victoria said, attempting to snatch her arm out of Tameka's grip. "My business is my business."

"Wrong," Tameka said and smacked Victoria across her face. "Your business is my business, you little whore."

"Fo' real you got to go. Kenneth will be home any minute," Victoria said in a pleading tone.

"Fuck Kenneth! My bad, you already did that," Tameka said sarcastically.

Throwing Victoria on the living room couch, Tameka pulled at her pants.

"Stop Tameka! Stop! What are you doing?" Victoria screamed.

"Shut up bitch! You gave that nigga my pussy and now you frontin on me. Hell fucking nah!" Tameka said, wrestling with Victoria.

Tameka was desperately trying to remove Victoria's pants when Kenneth entered his house. He stood frozen in the doorway, and blinked repeatedly as he witnessed Victoria struggling to fight off Tameka's unwelcomed advances. It about thirty seconds for Kenneth to snap out of his daze. He rushed Tameka.

"Bitch, what the fuck is your problem?" Kenneth shouted, throwing Tameka across the room.

"Nigga, you done fucked up now," Tameka said, pulling out her straight razor. "C'mon nigga, come get some o' this!"

Kenneth had left his gun in his truck. Glancing around, he scanned his living room for a weapon.

"Fo' real, put the razor down, Tameka. Don't hurt Kenneth."

Tameka's focus switched from Kenneth to Victoria. She angrily snarled, "You done lost yo mind taking up for this limp dick muthafucka! I'm—"

Tameka didn't finish her sentence. Kenneth tackled her to the ground, causing the razor to fall from her hand. They wrestled on the ground until Tameka kneed Kenneth in his groin.

"You bitch!" Kenneth said, groaning.

Victoria had been sitting on the floor watching the action. Tameka saw Victoria run for the razor and also ran for the razor. Victoria beat Tameka to the blade. She picked it up and Tameka hit her with a right hand to the back of her head. Victoria dropped the razor, and Tameka picked it up.

"You stupid-ass, bitch! You love this nigga more than me. I'm a show yo ass sump'n."

Kenneth was still balled up on the floor when Tameka walked over to him. Tameka raised the razor and Kenneth kicked her in the right knee. She collapsed in pain. Kenneth scrambled to his feet. He stared at Victoria as if thinking.

"Call the police," Kenneth said, getting up on wobbly legs.

Before Victoria could make it to the phone, she heard Kenneth screamed in pain. She turned around in time to see Kenneth falling to the floor.

"No!" she screamed, running out the living room.

"Yeah, how you like that?" Tameka said, watching blood leaking from where she sliced Kenneth on his leg. "You just couldn't leave us alone. You just had to steal my bitch from me. Now you gonna pay the ultimate price."

Tameka raised the razor and Victoria shouted, "Tameka, stop!"

Tameka turned around and saw Victoria holding a 9mm pointed at her.

"What you gonna do with that?" Tameka asked, walking toward Victoria. "Go ahead, shoot. I ain't got shit to live for."

"Stop Tameka! Fo' real, please stop!"

Tameka kept getting closer. She got within five feet of Victoria and made a jump to get at her.

Boom!

Tameka fell to the floor and was motionless. Victoria ran over to Kenneth.

"Baby, are you all right?"

"I am now," Kenneth said, taking the gun from Victoria. "The power of the pussy is a dangerous thing."

The End

THE *Hood*
IS MOBILE...

Our titles interlace action, crime, and the urban lifestyle depicting the harsh realities of life on the streets. Call it street literature, urban drama, we call it hip-hop literature. This exciting genre features fast-paced action, gritty ghetto realism, and social messages about the high price of the street life style.

DEAD AND STINKIN'
STEPHEN HEWETT

A GOOD DAY TO DIE
JAMES HENDRICKS

WHEN LOVE TURNS TO HATE
SHARRON DOYLE

**IF IT AIN'T ONE THING
IT'S ANOTHER**
SHARRON DOYLE

WOMAN'S CRY
VANESSA MARTIR

BLACKOUT
JERRY LaMOTHE
ANTHONY WHYTE

HUSTLE HARD
BLAINE MARTIN

A BOOGIE DOWN STORY
KEISHA SEIGNIOUS

CRAVE ALL LOSE ALL
ERICK S GRAY

LOVE AND A GANGSTA
ERICK S GRAY

AMERICA'S SOUL
ERICK S GRAY

LIES OF A REAL HOUSEWIFE
ANGELA STANTON

Mail us a List of the titles you would like include $14.95 per Title + shipping charges $3.95 for one book & $1.00 for each additional book. Make all checks payable to: Augustus Publishing 33 Indian Rd. NY, NY 10034

HARD WHITE
SHANNON HOLMES
ANTHONY WHYTE

STREET CHIC
ANTHONY WHYTE

BOOTY CALL *69
ERICK S GRAY

POWER OF THE P
JAMES HENDRICKS

STREETS OF NEW YORK VOL. 1
ERICK S GRAY, ANTHONY WHYTE
MARK ANTHONY, SHANNON HOLMES

STREETS OF NEW YORK VOL. 2
ERICK S GRAY, ANTHONY WHYTE
MARK ANTHONY, K'WAN

STREETS OF NEW YORK VOL. 3
ERICK S GRAY, ANTHONY WHYTE
MARK ANTHONY, TREASURE BLUE

SMUT CENTRAL
BRANDON McCALLA

GHETTO GIRLS
ANTHONY WHYTE

GHETTO GIRLS TOO
ANTHONY WHYTE

GHETTO GIRLS 3:
SOO HOOD
ANTHONY WHYTE

GHETTO GIRLS IV:
YOUNG LUV
ANTHONY WHYTE

SPOT RUSHERS
BRANDON McCALLA

IT CAN HAPPEN
IN A MINUTE
S.M. JOHNSON

LIPSTICK DIARIES
CRYSTAL LACEY WINSLOW
VARIOUS FEMALE AUTHORS

LIPSTICK DIARIES 2
WAHIDA CLARK
VARIOUS FEMALE AUTHORS